'We'll be seeing Roman promised with a smile before he straightened up.

'Sam won't be seeing you, and neither will I. To be blunt, Mr O'Hagan, I don't actually like you very much.'

'Actually, Miss Smith, I'm not wild about you either...but I think you'll find you'll be seeing a lot more of me...!'

Kim Lawrence lives on a farm in rural Anglesey. She runs two miles daily and finds this an excellent opportunity to unwind and seek inspiration for her writing! It also helps her keep up with her husband, two active sons, and the various stray animals which have adopted them. Always a fanatical consumer of fiction, she is now equally enthusiastic about writing. She loves a happy ending!

Recent titles by the same author:

HER BABY SECRET
THE BLACKMAILED BRIDE
THE GROOM'S ULTIMATUM
THE GREEK TYCOON'S WIFE
AT THE PLAYBOY'S PLEASURE
THE ITALIAN PLAYBOY'S PROPOSITION
THE SPANIARD'S LOVE-CHILD

THE ITALIAN'S SECRET BABY

BY
KIM LAWRENCE

MILLS & BOON®

All the characters in this book have no existence outside the imagination of the author, and have no relation whatsoever to anyone bearing the same name or names. They are not even distantly inspired by any individual known or unknown to the author, and all the incidents are pure invention.

First published in Great Britain 2004
Harlequin Mills & Boon Limited,
Eton House, 18-24 Paradise Road, Richmond, Surrey TW9 1SR

© Kim Lawrence 2004

ISBN 0-263-83750-5

Set in Times Roman 10½ on 11¾ pt.
01-0604-50252

Printed and bound in Spain
by Litografia Rosés, S.A., Barcelona

CHAPTER ONE

'I THOUGHT you were going to be late,' his PA said as Roman O'Hagan walked into the empty conference room.

'I don't know if I've ever mentioned this, Alice, but you have a very uptight attitude to timekeeping,' Roman observed, shrugging off his jacket and laying it across the back of a chair. 'And in case it's slipped your mind, I'm the boss so I'm allowed to be late.'

Alice, who had worked for him for four years and had no recollection of him ever being late during that time, planted a cup of coffee in front of him on the long polished table.

'Well, *boss*, I managed to get us on the four-thirty Dublin flight.'

'Excellent.' Swivelling his chair around, Roman stretched his long legs out comfortably in front of him and added with a pained grimace, 'Which is more than I can say for this coffee! And I use the word in the loosest possible sense.' He stared down suspiciously at the pale brown liquid in his cup.

'It's decaff, and in case it's slipped your mind making coffee is not part of my job description. I do it simply because I have a nice nature.'

'I'm a lucky man,' Roman returned, deadpan.

'Yes, you are.' She paused by the door. 'By the way, your brother rang.'

'Did he leave a message?'

'Not for you.'

Roman's darkly defined brows lifted at the cryptic response. He was as sure as he could be without written proof that his brother, Luca, had a lot to do with the fact his assistant had gone down a dress size during the past couple of months.

It was getting hard to maintain a tactful silence on the subject of his brother not being the marrying kind—*Alice was*.

'He said he'd call back.'

The conference call started off really well, but went rapidly downhill once the second speaker came on the line.

How is it possible for anyone to talk for so long and say absolutely nothing?

Roman interrupted the interminable flow. The response was if anything even more rambling. It also cleared up the question of whether this well-paid individual had grasped the problem or done the necessary research—*he hadn't*!

Roman listened with a half-smile as the man's junior managed to bail out his boss without making it obvious that was what he was doing; he also predicted and responded to the two further questions Roman had planned to ask.

Roman wouldn't forget his name.

'So you think the European market is ready for a project of this—' Before he got to complete his question a female voice, a low, husky, very attractive female voice interrupted him.

'Excuse me, but am I speaking to Mr O'Hagan?'

'Who is that?'

'A Mr *Roman* O'Hagan?'

'How on earth…? I'm afraid this is a private…'

'I'm trying to contact a Mr O'Hagan. Could you tell me who I'm speaking to?'

That combination of selective deafness and persistence,

even if she did have an extraordinarily sexy voice, was going to get wearing very quickly, Roman decided.

F. O'Hagan and Sons had recently been held up as a shining example of firms that employed a higher number than average of females in top-management-level jobs, but none of them was taking part in this conference call today.

Roman didn't have the faintest idea who this woman was or how she had turned up smack bang in the middle of a highly sensitive discussion. He doubted if it was worth the bother of finding out.

Who did people blame for cock-ups before the advent of computers?

'I don't know how you got on this line...' Roman stopped. The lazy smile that formed on his wide sensual mouth held more than a hint of self-derision. Could it be, he wondered, that his display of uncharacteristic tolerance might not be totally unconnected with the fact the gate-crasher had a very attractive voice? In his head those smoky, sultry tones were inextricably linked with long legs, seductive lips and long blonde hair.

'Well, don't ask me! Perhaps it was your turn to fob me off?' came the bitter speculation. 'I've been put through to every other blessed person in the building!'

Goodbye sultry seductress, hello schoolteacher. Oh, well, the harmless fantasy had been nice while it lasted.

'I've been fobbed off and made to wait—'

'Do you mind hanging up? This is a private and confidential discussion.' Some men might like their women bossy—each to his own, that was his motto—only his own taste didn't run in that direction.

Unlike his top management people from across Europe who were hanging on every word of this conversation, the woman on the other end of the line didn't appear to realise that when the head of O'Hagan Construction used this tone the conversation was at an end.

'I've not the *slightest* interest in your discussion,' the owner of the husky voice promised him with considerable feeling.

Roman expelled his breath in a hiss of frustrated irritation. He flicked his wrist, exposing the metal banded watch. 'That's what all the industrial spies say, however—'

'Is that meant to be a joke?' the voice demanded, dropping several degrees below freezing. 'Because I have to tell you I'm really not in the mood. And I warn you if I have to listen to ''The Blue Danube'' one more time I shall not be responsible for the consequences,' she warned darkly. 'Do you want a gibbering female running naked through town on your conscience—?'

'It would depend on the female—'

'I'm so glad you find this amusing.'

'Do you ever let anyone finish what they're attempting to say?'

'For heaven's sake, I'm not asking for a personal audience with the Pope, I just want to speak to Mr O'Hagan.'

Roman leaned his head into his hands. 'Obviously she doesn't—'

'I think it's extremely bad manners to speak about someone in the third person when they…me…I can hear every word you're saying! As I've already explained to *umpteen* people, this really is important.'

Roman's lips twisted in a cynical grimace. Hands clasped behind his head, he leaned back into his upholstered leather chair.

'I'd be surprised if it wasn't,' he observed drily.

The people who wanted to speak to him inevitably considered what they had to say was important. Ninety per cent of them wanted to make him a fortune; all they needed was just a bit of his own money to get their schemes up and running. Very few of these cranks got to tell him about their projects in person because as a rule his calls were screened.

This was one of the concessions he'd been forced to make to security after he'd badly misjudged a situation. He'd turned up at the office one morning to find his stalker—a mild middle-aged woman whom he, in his wisdom, had considered sad, not dangerous—had already been there complete with kitchen knife delusions and a hostage in the shape of his terrified PA.

Alice still had the scar. Unconsciously his hand went to his face. Fortunately you couldn't see hers, but his own reminded him of his poor judgement every time he looked in the mirror.

'*Alice*,' he yelled, swivelling his chair around and positioning it to face the open door, 'I've got a damned crank on this line, can you do something about it?'

'I'm not a crank!' The disembodied voice filled the room with husky outrage.

'Fair enough,' he drawled. 'However, you are on a private line so hang up! If you have a message there are channels you can go through.'

'Haven't you been listening to *anything* I've said? I don't have time for *channels*. Has anyone ever told you that you're an extremely rude man?'

'This has been said, but rarely to my face.'

'*Very ironic*,' came the blighting response. 'But I'm not talking to your face. If I was I might be able…listen, *are* you Mr O'Hagan?'

'I am Roman O'Hagan. If you're not going to hang up, do you think you might get round some time in the next hour to telling me who the hell you are? If only so that I can make sure you never have an opportunity to harangue me in the future.'

This threat produced an audible sigh at the other end. 'Well, I do think you might have said so straight away instead of wasting my time.'

'Wasting *your* time…?' Roman hoped his silent and invisible executives would stay quiet.

'My name is Scarlet Smith.'

Scarlet… Roman found he was thinking long legs again and, definitely, blonde hair. Not that any amount of hair or legs would make the woman who had this runaway mouth someone he'd ask for a second date…or even a first!

'I manage the crèche at the university.'

So he'd been halfway right with schoolteacher.

'Your mother is officially opening it today.'

'My mother is in Rome.' Roman stopped, having a vague recollection, now that he thought about it, of his mother having mentioned she was interrupting her holiday with her family to fly back and fulfil some commitment…it could well have been this one.

'No, she's in my office, and I'm afraid she isn't very well.'

Roman levered his long-limbed frame into an upright position, his languid air vanishing. 'What's happened?'

'I don't mean to alarm you—'

'Well, you are, so get to the point,' he advised tersely.

'Your mother fainted a little while ago. She seems better now.'

His mother didn't faint. 'What does the doctor say?' Roman asked, settling his loose Italian-designed jacket smoothly across his broad shoulders.

'She hasn't seen a doctor.'

Roman picked up on the defensive note that had entered the attractive voice and his brows drew together in a disapproving straight line.

'Why the hell not?' he demanded. 'I need the car,' he

added seamlessly as he turned to his attentively hovering PA, who, like all good assistants, knew when to say nothing. 'And cancel all my appointments for the rest of the morning, then tell Phil to meet me at the university.'

'Our flight…?'

'Cancel.'

'What if Dr O'Connor is busy—?'

Roman turned his head and looked at her; Alice took the hint.

'Right, I'll tell him to drop everything, though that might be hard if he's in the middle of heart surgery.'

'He's a medical man; he doesn't operate,' Roman retorted. 'Just explain to him what's happened, Alice, and tell him to bring his bag.'

'Your mother wouldn't let me call a doctor or an ambulance.'

Roman turned around as if to face the bleating voice. '*Let you?* She was unconscious,' he derided scornfully.

'For less than a minute.'

Roman knew when he heard someone covering their back; there was nothing he despised more. He came down hard on people who preferred to shift the blame because they lacked the guts to carry the can for their own mistakes.

'Let me tell you, *Miss Smith*, if my mother suffers a broken fingernail that could have been avoided if you had called for medical assistance I'll sue the pants off you and your university!' he promised darkly before cutting her off.

His PA was unable to remain silent. 'Really, you can be so mean!'

'What is this? Sisterly solidarity?'

'I don't think you realise how much you terrify people,' she reproved, shaking her head.

'No, Alice, I know *exactly* how much I terrify people.'

He gave a white wolfish smile. 'It's the secret behind my success.'

'Nonsense,' returned Alice. 'The secret of your success is you live for your work and don't have a life,' she observed disapprovingly. 'You lack balance.'

'A little more terror, Alice, and a little less lip would be appreciated,' Roman drawled.

'That poor girl is probably crying her eyes out.'

'Pardon me but I don't empathise with incompetence, especially when that incompetence puts my family in danger,' he explained grimly.

Contrary to Alice's prediction, the 'poor girl' in question was neither terrified nor crying. She was walking down a university corridor where people who would normally have called out a cheery greeting took one look at her usually sunny face and changed their minds.

Others stared curiously when she walked past practising out loud—the acoustics were excellent—one of the cutting home truths she would like to deliver personally to Mr Roman O'Hagan.

'Get to the point,' he'd said. What did he think she'd been trying to do while he'd been cracking jokes at her expense?

Of course she should have called for an ambulance, she knew that—did he think she didn't know that?

David Anderson, the university's vice-chancellor, looked incredibly relieved as she walked through the door.

'I thought you were only going to be a second, Scarlet?' he said, drawing her a little to one side and out of earshot of the pale-faced woman sitting in the chair.

'How is she?' Scarlet asked, responding to his hand signals to keep her voice low.

'Better than she was, I think. She wants me to ask her driver to bring her car around.'

'I wouldn't bother, David; her son is on his way over,' she revealed casually.

On the whole, and considering how stressed David was already, Scarlet didn't see much point explaining that the millionaire property developer in question was in a very vengeful and litigious mood.

Obviously threats were part and parcel of Roman O'Hagan's *modus operandi*. Scarlet knew the type; she had suffered in silence at the hands of bullies during a lot of her school years. Years of unhappiness that she could have been spared if she had realised earlier that all you had to do with a bully was show them you weren't scared—*even if you were*!

It hadn't been bravery in her last year at school that had made her turn around and tell her gang of tormentors exactly what she thought of them, it had been simply a matter of reaching the end of her tether.

The experience had left Scarlet with a loathing of bullies and a determination to never again put herself in the role of victim. Every time she replayed the phone conversation in her head she felt her anger rising. How dared he threaten her? It wasn't just *what* he had said, it was the *way* he had said it.

And that *voice*; she recalled the inexplicable reaction she had had to the low drawl. Incredibly it had actually produced a physical response. She had reacted to it like a cat whose fur had been stroked the wrong way, her skin literally prickling in an uncomfortable way.

He had the sort of voice that could make an eviction notice sound sexy.

The vice-chancellor shot her a look of annoyed disbelief, which she pretended not to notice.

'You called Roman O'Hagan after she *specifically* asked you not to?' He groaned.

'Did she?'

'I know she did, Scarlet, because I was there at the time and I heard what she said, not once, but twice.'

'So maybe she did,' Scarlet conceded. 'But she also *specifically* asked us not to call a medic or ambulance,' she reminded him. 'And I thought that was wrong too.'

'She's a very important woman; we can't go around ignoring her wishes.'

'You didn't; I did.'

David looked somewhat mollified by this reminder. 'That's true.'

'Just call me Scarlet the scapegoat,' she suggested cheerfully.

David shot her a reproachful look from under his half-moon specs. 'I'll just go and organise someone to meet Mr O'Hagan.'

A three-man job at least, Scarlet mused scornfully: one person to grovel, another to sprinkle rose petals in his path and, last but not least, one to stroke the guy's massive ego. She for one didn't envy anyone the task of being nice to him. Even allowing for his concern over his mother, the mega-rich playboy had come across as a nasty bully of a man. Being rich, in her view, did not give anyone carte blanche to be rude.

'Where's a spare red carpet when you need one?'

David shot her a wary look. 'I hope you weren't rude to him.'

Scarlet adopted a puzzled expression, her eyes wide and innocent.

'Don't look at me like that, Scarlet, it worries me. I've known you since you were six years old,' he reminded her drily.

'Why would I be rude to the man? I rang to tell him his mother wasn't well.'

'Hummph.' David left her with a firm admonition not to take any further unilateral decisions if she wanted to keep her job.

'Are you feeling any better?' Scarlet asked, approaching the slim, elegant figure who was dressed in a soft apricot suit that hinted tastefully at a good cleavage.

'Much better, thank you,' Natalia O'Hagan replied in her soft, attractive Italian accent.

She didn't look nearly old enough to have a son the age of Roman O'Hagan.

Unless he had begun his infamous playboy lifestyle when he was still at school he had to be in his early thirties at least to have fitted in all the beautiful women who had reputedly enjoyed his admiration. As aloof and arrogant as he was widely reported to be, he was rarely photographed without some lush beauty gazing adoringly up into his face.

Scarlet smiled at Natalia. She had taken to the older woman immediately. Unlike her son she came across as a warm, genuine woman with no airs and graces. Just thinking about the vile son with his hateful, sarcastic drawl sent a shudder of antipathy down Scarlet's spine.

Maybe Roman O'Hagan had inherited his arrogance from the paternal side of the equation. It was quite a combination of genes, Italian and Irish, Scarlet reflected, and on the evidence so far she'd say the result of that fusion had produced a person who lacked the charm of the Irish and the charisma of the Italians.

Despite her reassurance as she lifted the glass of water, there was a visible tremor in the older woman's hand.

'Let me,' Scarlet said, taking the glass from her and placing it back on her own desk.

On closer inspection she could see that the scary bluish tinge had receded from around the older woman's lips. This was good news, but despite these small signs of improvement the woman still looked far from well.

'Can I get you anything else?'

Natalia O'Hagan lifted her head, her lips formed a weak smile, but she didn't appear able to respond to the question.

Scarlet's anxiety increased. She privately called herself every sort of weak idiot for not having stood her ground in the first place and rung for a doctor straight off as she'd wanted.

In that at least her wretched son had been right.

She could have insisted, but when the university bigwigs, who had tagged along with David for the official opening ceremony of the crèche, had overruled her, what had she done? She'd meekly rolled over.

As far as the powers that be were concerned they weren't going to risk upsetting the woman whose generous donation had been responsible for the refurbishment and extension of the crèche facilities, not to mention the new state-of-the art IT building. And Natalia O'Hagan had managed to make it quite clear despite her weak condition, that she did not want a doctor.

That was fine and their call to make, but where were they now, those men and women in suits who knew better? Their absence from the vicinity was pretty conspicuous.

Scarlet had only been half joking when she'd called herself a scapegoat. If anything went wrong it wasn't difficult to figure out who would be left to carry the can, especially if Roman O'Hagan had anything to do with it. She couldn't see the men and women in suits leaping up to take responsibility.

'Won't you let me get someone down from Occupational Health, at least—?' Scarlet began, only to be cut off by an impatient, slightly imperious nod of the smooth dark head.

'You sound just like my sons.'

Scarlet had no control over the expression of horror that spread across her face. *'Me?'*

'You know, I consider myself a lucky woman,' Natalia revealed. 'Two sons who I love dearly, and they are so good to me. But,' she explained with a shake of her head, 'they are both ridiculously overprotective. Roman is possibly the worst.

'He has a terrible habit of thinking he knows what is best,' Natalia continued ruefully. 'If I'd let him he'd run my life, I swear he would.'

'You have to stand up to him!'

Natalia's delicate brow lifted at the heat of Scarlet's stern declaration.

Scarlet coloured self-consciously and forced her expression to relax. 'I suppose it's a son's job to be protective of his mother. I expect mine will one day,' she added lightly.

'You have a son?' Liquid dark eyes scanned Scarlet's slim figure. She was wearing her usual work garb, jeans and one of the bright child-friendly tee shirts all the helpers in the crèche wore. It had been suggested that, as the manager of the centre, she ought to wear something more in fitting with her management role, but Scarlet, a hands-on sort of manager, had stuck to her guns and her tee shirt.

'Goodness, you look so young, or maybe that's just me getting old.'

'You're not old.'

'When I look at those little ones I feel…' She suddenly went very still as she looked through the plate-glass partition to the room beyond. It should have been empty; the children were enjoying the party on the lawn. 'That child—what is his name?'

It was a casual enough question, but *casual* in Scarlet's experience didn't equate with the lines of tension bracketing the older woman's soft mouth or the tortured twisting of the hands clasped in her lap.

'Which one? We've got quite a few here. Should you lie down, perhaps…?' she suggested tentatively. 'If you're not feeling well?'

'I'm feeling fine.' The strained smile she produced to prove the point did nothing to soothe Scarlet's fears. 'The little boy I'm talking about is the one who gave me the flowers? The one sitting there.'

Scarlet followed the direction of the ashen-faced woman's strangely haunted gaze as Natalie nodded through the glass partition that separated Scarlet's office from the big, newly equipped play room, towards a small dark-haired figure sitting cross-legged on the floor.

Sam was meant to be outside with the other children watching the magician they'd engaged as entertainment. With the party in full swing he had obviously managed to slip away unnoticed. Sam was a very resourceful child.

He had wanted to finish his jigsaw earlier, and when he wanted something, as she knew to her cost, he could show remarkable focus. His little face was a mask of concentration as he slotted the final piece into a complicated wooden jigsaw and gave a triumphant smile.

'Sam,' Scarlet replied, a puzzled frown forming between her brows as she registered the throb of emotion in the other woman's attractively accented voice.

'I hope I didn't alarm him.'

'Sam takes most things in his stride,' Scarlet returned honestly.

'I thought he might,' came the puzzling dry rejoinder. 'His mother…does she work at the university?'

'Sam's my son, the one I mentioned.' Scarlet was trying very hard not to glow too obviously with pride. 'One of the perks of running the university crèche is I get to bring him to work with me.'

This hadn't happened by accident. Early on Scarlet had realised to leave Sam on a daily basis would be too painful, not necessarily for the child, who possessed an adaptable and sunny personality, but for herself.

'*You?*'

Scarlet endured with equanimity the astonished, searching scrutiny that came her way. The reaction didn't surprise her. Sam was an exceptionally beautiful child, and Scarlet knew the only thing exceptional about herself was her ordinariness, but even so the softly breathed, '*Unbelievable!*' did bring a faint flush to her pale cheeks.

As if she realised her lapse in manners, a flicker of something akin to embarrassment flickered across the beautiful features of the VIP guest.

'And how old is Sam?'

'He was three in April.'

'He seems very advanced for his age.'

'Sam is quick,' Scarlet agreed, unable to stifle a flicker of parental pride at this praise.

'You and your husband must be very proud of him.'

'I'm not married.' Even in this enlightened age Scarlet was used to her single motherhood producing disapproval in varying degrees, but the inexplicable flicker of relief she saw in Natalia's brown eyes was not a reaction she'd encountered before.

It only lasted a moment and Scarlet almost immediately put it down to a trick of the light or her imagination. After all, she asked herself, why would her being unmarried make a total stranger relieved?

'Then Sam's father…?'

'There's just me and Sam and we like it that way,' Scarlet explained cheerfully.

CHAPTER TWO

'But it must be hard for a woman alone?'

'One-parent families are not exactly unusual.'

'But you've *never* been married?'

Scarlet, who was beginning to feel puzzled with the older woman's pursuit of the subject, shook her head. 'Never.' This might be a good time to change the subject and admit she had contacted the tyrannical son.

'Listen, Mrs O'Hagan—'

'Natalia, please, my dear.'

'*Natalia,* I know you asked me not to.' Scarlet took a deep breath and made a clean breast of it. 'The thing is I called Mr O'Hagan…that is your son, the control freak one,' she explained unhappily.

'I don't blame you being angry with me,' she continued, 'but I really did think that someone should know—' Scarlet stopped in response to a cool hand laid on her arm.

'I'm not angry with you, child.'

Scarlet gave a sigh of relief. 'I'm glad about that.'

'Did you speak to Roman yourself? I ask,' she added, 'because I have a problem doing so myself sometimes.' She gave a light laugh. 'He is guarded zealously.'

You can say that again!

'I did manage to, *eventually*,' Scarlet admitted with a guarded smile.

There was something in the other woman's manner…she couldn't quite put her finger on it, but Scarlet couldn't shake the feeling that she was missing something.

'My, you must be a determined girl, or have special access that I don't?' Her laughter had a forced sound to it.

'I could have done with it, but I had to fall back on my natural talent—I'm stubborn.'

Natalia nodded; her expression suggested her thoughts had already moved on. 'I sometimes think this security business has got out of hand, you know. Since the stalker affair Roman is not a very accessible person, but no doubt you know that.'

'Stalker?' Scarlet queried, pausing to briefly wonder why his mother would assume she knew anything at all about her son.

'Oh, I'm sure you read about it. That woman who became obsessed with him? It was about four years ago.'

Scarlet shook her head. She was not about to explain that four years ago her world had narrowed to the bedside of her dying sister.

'Perhaps you were out of the country?'

'Not likely,' Scarlet returned. 'I get seasick and have a phobia of flying.'

'How inconvenient. Actually it was covered quite widely in the papers—this woman developed a thing about Roman.'

'An ex-girlfriend?' That figured. Any woman who went out with him had to be slightly unbalanced to begin with.

'Well, no, that's the thing, they had never actually met, but she became convinced they had a relationship. She wrote to him, telephoned him, sent him gifts…initially Roman felt sorry for her and thought if he ignored her she'd go away. Things came to a head when he arrived at the office one morning to find her holding his PA at knife-point.'

'Gracious!' Scarlet gasped, her eyes widening in horror. 'Was anyone hurt?'

'Roman managed to talk her into letting Alice go and

apparently she was going to hand over the knife when the police arrived. The woman panicked and became quite frenzied. Roman and Alice both got injured, Alice badly. Fortunately they both recovered.'

'That must have been very traumatic.'

'It was, though Roman was more concerned that he had unwittingly put someone else's life at risk. Oh, I know it wasn't his fault.' Scarlet, who hadn't been going to suggest anything of the sort, remained, silent. 'But Roman has a very overdeveloped sense of responsibility.'

Scarlet smiled politely and wondered privately how much a mother's natural bias had coloured this version of events. Certainly this caring, sensitive paragon didn't sound much like the man the newspapers were so fond of writing about or the one she had spoken to earlier!

'Roman admires a woman with spirit.'

Roman manages to hide his admiration pretty well. 'Really…?' she responded, not sure what else she was supposed to say to this apparently irrelevant comment.

'And what did my son have to say for himself?'

Beyond threaten to sue the socks off me? 'Oh, we didn't really chat,' she responded lightly.

'Well, you'll be able to get reacquainted properly when he arrives. The years have changed him, you know, my dear.'

The turn of phrase struck Scarlet as distinctly odd, but she was so relieved that the older woman appeared resigned that her son was coming to collect her that she didn't comment on it.

'Scarlet.' David appeared at the door. 'Could I have a word for a moment? Mrs O'Hagan, it's good to see you looking so much better.'

Now that he said so, Scarlet too saw that the older

woman had perked up considerably. 'I'll be right back,' she promised.

Actually she wasn't right back because David had been informed that Roman O'Hagan was in the building and, as he put it, thought that, 'a more *senior* member of staff should be here when he arrives. No reflection on your abilities, Scarlet, but as a sign of respect.'

Scarlet gave him no argument. 'I think it's the least he would expect,' she agreed.

It suited her down to the ground not to be there when the bullying millionaire put in an appearance. If she had to be nice to him she'd choke.

'I might take that time owing me and nip off now with Sam, unless you want me to hang around?'

Roman ran his long fingers through the gleaming strands of his dark hair in a gesture of impatience. The same impatience was etched in the strong, symmetrical lines of his darkly handsome face as he looked down at his mother.

'Yes, it *was* necessary for me to bring Philip; he is your doctor.'

'And as I have told him, I fainted, nothing more. You are fussing like an old woman, Roman,' she told her son scornfully. Graciously she extended her arm for the suited figure to apply a blood-pressure cuff. 'Normal?' she asked as the medic removed the stethoscope from his ears.

The doctor nodded. 'If all my patients were this healthy I'd be out of business,' he told her cheerfully.

Natalia shot her son a triumphant look. 'I told you so,' she murmured complacently.

'But you will carry out further tests?' Roman addressed his query to his friend.

'I could, but—'

'Do them.'

Natalia gave a sigh of exasperation. 'This is exactly why I didn't want them to ring you. You come rushing here when I'm sure you have a million more important things to do.'

'Several million things, actually,' Roman corrected, the corners of his wide, sensual mouth lifting in a sarcastic smile. 'Naturally all *much* more important than my mother's health.'

'Well, I'm glad to see that family is still important to you, Roman.'

One dark brow quirked as, with slightly narrowed eyes, he scanned his mother's face. Never slow when it came to reading between the lines, he asked, 'Am I missing something here?'

'You spoke to Scarlet on the phone, I believe.'

'Scarlet—the blonde?'

'She is not blonde. Though I suppose she might have been blonde when you knew her, though women usually go from brunette to blonde, not the other way.'

'I don't and didn't know her.'

'Well, why did you say she was blonde?'

'She sounded blonde.'

His mother looked at him blankly. '*Sounded* blonde? Really, Roman, do not insult my intelligence,' she rebuked coldly.

'Did she say I knew her?' He was accustomed to women trying to get to him, but if this one thought she could use his mother to do so she could think again!

'Relax, Roman. She hardly mentioned you at all, which,' Natalia added heavily, 'is hardly surprising,' his mother reproached. 'This must have been a very painful experience for her.'

'Told you I threatened her, did she? Well, she deserved it. How could anyone not have the wit to get medical help?'

Natalia stared at her son for a moment, then appeared to

come to a decision. She turned to the doctor. 'Philip, dear, do you mind? I've got something I need to say to Roman.'

The doctor clicked closed his case. 'Of course, no problem.'

Roman flashed his friend a brief nod. 'We'll see you back at the clinic in fifteen minutes.'

Other than give an exasperated click of her tongue, Natalia did not respond to his comments.

'Is this going to take long, Mother?' Roman asked as the door closed.

'Should I have made an appointment?' Natalia enquired spikily. 'You may be a *very* important man, but you might want to remember that you're running the company because *I* persuaded your father to retire.'

It had actually been his father's heart attack that had persuaded him and his equally reluctant brother to put their careers on hold and divide their father's responsibilities. The injection of fresh blood and new ideas had produced results that had seen the O'Hagan family's fortunes grow rapidly.

Unfortunately the success had increased, not lessened, the tension between father and sons.

'I'll pass on the fact that two minutes ago you were telling me my time was too important to spend it doing anything as frivolous as rushing to my mother's side.'

'Don't change the subject, Roman.'

'I wouldn't dare if I knew what it was. Are you going to tell me any time soon what exactly I've done?' Roman drawled. 'I know all the signs,' he added grimly. 'I've searched my conscience and nothing immediately springs to mind. I must admit I'm curious.'

Natalia's eyes flashed as her son gave a smile that was both cynical and charming in equal measure. She didn't smile back, but instead snatched from his fingers the pen he was idly doodling with and banged it down on the blotter.

'Don't do that.' Her sons had inherited their father's Irish charm, her own dark Italian looks and, sadly, neither had very many scruples when it came to using either to get what they wanted. Roman had been getting pretty much what he wanted all his life, with one notable exception.

A frown formed between his dark, strongly delineated brows as Roman studied his mother's face. 'Has something happened? Dad…?'

Natalia heard the anxiety enter his deep voice, roughening the velvet-smooth tone, and immediately shook her head reassuringly. Eyes trained on his face, she took a deep, shuddering sigh. *'Scarlet Smith.'* She flung the name like an accusation.

'The woman with the smart tongue and the bad attitude who is not a blonde. If you want to know anything else you're going to have to go elsewhere because that about exhausts my knowledge of the woman.'

Natalia searched her son's face for a moment before her body sagged in relief. 'You didn't know, then.' She sighed. 'I didn't think you could have,' she revealed.

'Didn't know and still don't,' he inserted drily.

'She must have changed her name, or maybe she gave you a false name?'

'Are we back on the not-blonde?'

'I don't approve of everything you do, Roman.'

Roman's expression became stoical as he prepared to endure one of his mother's lectures on his lifestyle with a modicum of patience—patience he would not have extended to anyone else who chose to criticise him.

'But I simply couldn't imagine you abandoning your responsibilities and letting your own son grow up not even knowing who you are.'

CHAPTER THREE

ROMAN, whose hard features had begun to relax into a rueful half-smile at his mother's initial comments, stiffened as she delivered her killer punchline.

'*Son!*' Pallor crept up under his even olive-toned Latin complexion. 'If that's your idea of a joke?' he grated.

'I'm hardly likely to joke about such a thing,' Natalia said. 'Look, I can see this must have come as a shock to you.'

'That's very understanding of you.' Roman's irony was wasted on his mother. 'I don't have a son and I've never met a...' his forehead creased as he tried to recall the non-blonde's name '...Scarlet Smith?'

'Yes, lovely girl.' She glanced across at her son and shook her head.

She watched with some sympathy as her son ground his teeth and stalked stiff-backed across the room, his whole manner screaming anger and frustration. She came up behind him and put her hand on his shoulder. Though she was five eleven in her heels, she had to tilt her head to look him in the face.

'Be honest, is this so impossible to believe?'

'Don't you think I'd know about it if I had a son?' he suggested, his tone deceptively mild.

Natalia gave a very Latin shrug. 'Only if the mother chose to tell you, Roman.'

'And always supposing I did actually make a habit—as you obviously believe—of going around impregnating women. Why the hell wouldn't she have told me? Why

27

struggle to bring up a child as a single parent?' A flicker of suspicion crossed his face. 'Or is she married?'

'You sleep with married women?'

Roman's head went back as he looked heavenwards, sending the dark hair he wore a little longer than was conventional against the collar of his pale shirt. 'No, I do not sleep with married women,' he replied between clenched white teeth.

'Never?'

A hissing sound of seething frustration escaped through Roman's teeth as his mother continued to look at him with an expression of disappointment.

'Not knowingly.'

'Ignorance is no defence in law, or so I've always understood. I accept you didn't know you had a child. Now you do. What are you going to do about it?' she challenged.

'For the last time, I do *not* have a child!'

Natalia gave an inflammatory sigh. 'Denial isn't going to get us anywhere.'

'I'm not in denial,' Roman thundered.

'Yes, you are, and there's no need to raise your voice, Roman, I'm not deaf.'

The bitterness died from his face as he saw the unexpected sparkle of tears in his mother's eyes. 'Sit down,' he insisted, his concern coming across as impatience.

'It must have been some story this woman spun you.' Roman's facial muscles tightened. 'You can normally spot a phoney a mile off. Didn't it strike you as odd that she told you, not me?'

'She didn't tell me anything at all. I gave her every opportunity, but in fact Scarlet pretended not to know you.'

A flicker of incomprehension crossed Roman's face. 'Then what the hell is this about?'

'I've seen the child, Roman, and he *is* you at the same age.'

Roman looked at her for a moment, his dark brows raised, before releasing an incredulous laugh.

'This isn't funny, Roman,' she reproached.

'No, it's not funny to see you so upset,' he agreed sombrely as he hunkered down beside his mother's chair. 'All right, this kid looks like I did,' he acceded lightly. 'But I don't know any Scarlet Smith, the only time I've spoken to her was on the phone, I promise you, and I never forget a name.'

His mother nodded. 'People change in four years. You have,' she added, a tinge of sadness in her eyes.

'Scarlet must have changed her name so that you couldn't find her, that would explain you not recognising her name.'

'That would seem a tad excessive, considering I wasn't looking for her.'

'Don't be flippant,' Natalia snapped.

'I know you'd like to be a grandmother, but I'm not going to pretend I've fathered a kid to oblige you.'

'You wouldn't say that if you'd seen the boy, Roman.'

'Do you think I wouldn't remember the name of a woman I slept with?' he demanded.

'If it was four years ago I'd say you could have some problem. There were a lot of women. I know I shouldn't have brought it up...but...'

'You're going to anyway.' Roman's expression was resigned.

'It's not a subject I enjoy discussing.'

'That makes two of us.'

Being deserted by your childhood sweetheart after the invitations for the wedding had been sent out was not an experience he particularly cared to relive on a regular basis, and that was what his mother was trying to remind him of now.

Making a total fool of himself was something a man was allowed to do *once* in his life. When he made marriage plans the next time his decision would not be based on a blind infatuation and starry-eyed fantasies of a happy-ever-after existence.

A marriage based on a mutual respect where neither partner would feel wounded or outraged if the other sought excitement outside the marriage bed was one that would stand a much better chance of survival in the long run.

Natalia determinedly ignored the dry rejoinder. 'What I'm saying is it's not as if you've never had a one-night stand.'

'Can we leave my sex life out of this? I can hardly be surprised strangers believe what they read about me in the tabloids when my own mother does. You're accusing me of indiscriminately fathering children! Do you *really* think I'm that stupid?' he demanded.

'Just go and see the boy, then you'll understand, Roman. That's all I'm asking you to do. Are you trying to tell me that it wouldn't bother you never to know your own son?'

'I don't have a son.'

'One hundred per cent sure?'

Roman's broad shoulders lifted; playing along was clearly the only way he was going to put an end to this once and for all. He gave a sigh. 'So where will I find the mother of my child?'

'Can't *you* see him?'

'Mr O'Hagan asked *expressly* to see you.'

'I really didn't do much.'

'Just what I said...' Dragging his attention from the text message he was reading David added smoothly, 'I told him that we work as a team here, but it seems your name must have stuck in his mother's mind and of course you spoke to him on the phone.'

'That must be it,' Scarlet agreed drily. Oh, God, it would be just her luck if the man had decided to follow up his complaint officially, but if he had there wasn't any reason he couldn't have mentioned it to David straight off.

'It's a very nice gesture.'

'Men like Roman O'Hagan don't make nice gestures unless there's something in it for them,' she responded cynically.

'And you number how many multimillionaires amongst your circle?'

'I don't, but Abby knew a few.' At least Abby's circle of friends had aspired to the millionaire lifestyle, though, as her sister had explained, not all had had the means to support it.

She saw the flicker of sympathy her bitter remark brought to David's face and added quickly, 'The problem is we're so short-staffed with this flu epidemic. I could do without gestures, kind or otherwise.'

'The longer you spend arguing with me…God, Scarlet, what are you wearing?'

David had been her honorary uncle since she was tiny. Scarlet was always scrupulous about not trading on the family friend thing, but unfortunately David didn't feel similarly inhibited when it came to passing the sort of personal comments he wouldn't get away with with other staff members.

'Borrowed. A baby threw up all over me.'

'Goes with the territory, I would imagine,' came the bracing observation. 'And you were the one who insisted on leaving an indecently well-paid job in the City to work with children,' he reminded her.

'Days like this make me wonder why.'

'No, you don't, you love every minute of it. I don't know why, but you do.'

Scarlet conceded his point with a grin. 'I suppose asking him to come back another day is out of the question?' David looked at her over his metal-rimmed half moon spectacles as though she'd lost her mind.

'Come back another day?'

Scarlet shrugged. 'I thought I'd ask.' She caught sight of her reflection in the full-length window. 'God,' she cried, wincing, 'I can't see him looking like a bag lady.'

'I've seen you looking better, but he's not here to ask you for a date, Scarlet, so I really don't see the problem here.'

'I'm representing the university,' she said weakly.

'If you'd been a member of the academic staff I could see your point,' David responded, treating her suggestion seriously.

'How lucky that I'm only a nursery nurse,' she said dead-pan.

'Exactly, and look on the bright side, he's not going to think you made any special efforts for him which should suit your egalitarian principles down to the ground.'

'Very funny,' Scarlet muttered.

'Now, the sooner you go get your shoulder patted, the sooner you get back to help the troops out.'

With a shrug she admitted defeat.

'Mr O'Hagan is in my office.' David turned in the op-posite direction.

'Aren't you coming too?' Scarlet protested with a frown.

'I have an important meeting. Has it occurred to you you might actually like the man?'

'No.'

'Then pretend.' It was not a request.

'Mr O'Hagan, can I have your autograph,' she mocked, assuming an expression of brainless adoration.

'See, you can do it when you try,' David approved, banging her on the shoulder. 'Now off you go and remember he's a very important friend to this university, Scarlet.'

Scarlet nodded meekly. 'I'll be very nice to him.'

It didn't seem a too extravagant promise to make, considering it shouldn't take Roman O'Hagan long to go through the motions of thanking her—at least she hoped not!

CHAPTER FOUR

ROMAN glanced at his watch, his eyes slightly narrowed. If he could get the Scarlet Smith thing sorted before lunch he could fly back out to Dublin and join Alice, who was already there.

That was the best scenario, but if things did run over he didn't begrudge the time, not if the end result made his mother happy. Not as happy as being a grandmother would, but his sense of filial duty had limits.

It did not cross his mind for one second that his mother was correct. There was no possibility he had fathered a child. He had been many things in his life, but careless was not one of them.

Not a man given to moody introspection he turned his mind to the pivotal meeting in Dublin later that evening.

Scarlet tapped on the door half hoping that nobody would reply to her timid knock. Nobody did, but the door, already half ajar, swung open. The man revealed standing there, running a long brown finger down the spine of a leather-bound book, seemed oblivious to her presence.

She cleared her throat and his head turned. Dark lashes lifted to reveal eyes that were one shade short of pitch-black and flecked with tiny golden lights. Scarlet's eyes slid away from the most piercing regard she had ever encountered.

She gulped as her heart made a concerted effort to escape the confines of her chest.

In profile he was perfect; an overused term but more than justified on this occasion. Face on, only a purist would have claimed the fine scar that ran from one razor-sharp cheekbone to just below his eye marred the effect.

Scarlet wasn't that purist!

Roman's immediate thought as he stared at the diminutive brown-haired figure hovering uncertainly in the doorway was, *there must be some mistake.* Realistically, he hadn't actually been expecting some blonde goddess with endless legs, but *this*?

The indentation between his eyebrows deepened, the woman he had spoken to on the phone had come across as gutsy and unafraid to speak her mind, not to mention bloody-minded, but this woman looked scared of her own shadow! She couldn't even meet his eyes!

He experienced an unexpected pang of disappointment.

'Mr O'Hagan…?' Scarlet repeated when he didn't respond.

Great, I've struck him dumb, but not with my ravishing beauty!

'Mr O'Hagan, I understand you wanted to speak to me?'

The voice emerging from the slight frame was right, unexpectedly deep and husky with a sexy little rasp, but everything else was wrong, including the scared way she was not quite looking him in the eye and the tongue-tied routine.

Nice voice, shame about everything else.

'Miss Smith?'

Scarlet nodded, and resisted the aggravating impulse to apologise for her appearance.

'Why don't you come in and sit down?'

'I'm fine here.'

He looked at her impatiently. 'I don't bite.'

She flushed at the satirical note in his voice and realised she must look an idiot standing there as if she was ready to run. Straightening her shoulders, Scarlet overcame the strange reluctance she was experiencing to close the door.

She'd been in the room before and it wasn't exactly cramped—her own office would have fitted in it ten times over—but she was experiencing an almost claustrophobic sensation that involved a tightening in the pit of her stomach and an overwhelming desire to turn and run.

The man was here to say thank you, not interrogate her, or even sue her, unless his mother had suffered a relapse? He didn't give a damn what she looked like, so why the sudden panic attack? She didn't subscribe to the populist celebrity culture and was not overawed or impressed just because someone had fame and money. She was neither shy nor lacking in confidence so her irrational nervousness on this occasion annoyed her.

'So, we meet at last.'

Head down, she nodded.

His mother had thought he had slept with this woman?

He repressed a fastidious wince as he checked out the fashion black spot she represented.

He knew women who could look good in the proverbial sack, but this woman wasn't one of that number. That tunic checked shirt thing almost reached her knees, but at least it covered most of the appalling, baggy track-suit joggers she had teamed it with. There was nothing intrinsically dreadful about the sensible flat leather shoes that completed the ensemble, but they didn't do anything to disguise the fact she was small and shapeless.

Who knew what lurked under the androgynous outfit? He, for one, felt no compelling urge to find out. Though he would have liked to bin the outrageously unattractive glasses she wore, which concealed most of her features, simply on the grounds that they were criminally ugly.

Scarlet stood there miserably while his veiled gaze moved over her. He was suitably enigmatic, but not enigmatic enough to prevent Scarlet getting the impression she hadn't lived up to the billing his mother had given her.

She gave a mental shrug…ah, well, she could live with that!

Standing next to him, even if she had been looking her best, she would have felt plain and unkempt. Six feet four inches, give or take an inch, of spectacular male perfection. He more than lived up to his billing. Unbelievably he was even better looking in the flesh than in print!

She responded on two levels to this discovery. On the one hand she was disappointed at being robbed of the opportunity to confide derisively to her friends, It's all airbrushing, you know, he's not nearly as attractive as he looks in the magazines!

On the other level she responded as any woman would being faced with the most sinfully sexy man she had ever seen—or even imagined seeing!

'Miss *Scarlet* Smith?' Smith was a common name; maybe this was the wrong one? She had the awkward slightly bemused manner of someone who had walked into the wrong office. 'You do know who I am?'

Didn't everyone? Her lowered gaze lifted. Maybe that was his problem; she hadn't asked for his autograph yet.

'I'm Scarlet. The vice-chancellor said you wanted to see me, Mr O'Hagan.'

A small derisive smile formed on her wide and expressive mouth; after their conversation she wasn't surprised to discover he was the type who thrived on public recognition and got irritated when he didn't receive it.

Well, promise to David or not, Mr. O'Hagan was about to learn she was not one of that creepy boot-licking number!

Her lips parted to ask if he wouldn't mind keeping it brief when his dark eyes locked onto her own.

Scarlet breathed in sharply and promptly forgot what she

was going to say. He really did have the most stunning eyes she'd ever seen, deep chocolate-brown, but not like the sweet milk chocolate she adored, but the dark variety that was too bitter for her palate. For a bemused moment she just stared into those dark, mesmerising topaz-flecked depths before pulling clear and closing her mouth with an audible click.

She gave a smile heavy on serene self-possession to correct any impression he might have got that she was a silly, drooling female. The last thing she wanted was to be heaped together with those adoring hordes.

Dating the rich and photogenic Roman O'Hagan had kick-started the career of many a would-be celebrity, and the women who weren't notorious before they shared the spotlight he lived in definitely were at the end of it!

However, considering her own involuntary fit of the fluttery females, Scarlet was now willing to consider that there might have been a few takers whose motives hadn't been purely mercenary.

Maybe it was the dark, smouldering thing, she mused, because, despite his mixed ancestry, Roman O'Hagan's features, colouring and innate elegance were very much that of the Latin male, as was the devastating raw masculinity he projected.

The clothes helped, of course, she decided scornfully as she put a mental price tag on the pale grey impeccably tailored grey suit he wore teamed with a black silky polo shirt open at the neck. Italian men were notoriously vain and she doubted this one could pass a reflective surface without checking himself out. The catty postscript made her feel better about being unable to find a flaw in his tall, broad-shouldered, narrow-hipped athletic frame.

Power, money and a good suit—maybe she wasn't so

different from everyone else easily impressed by the trappings of privilege…?

The suit or the man inside it? It's not his position on the social register that's got you hot!

Turning a deaf ear to the debate going on in her head, Scarlet turned her thoughts to her more immediate problem. After a moment's further deliberation she decided against shaking hands; if he didn't accept her hand she was going to look pretty silly and nothing about him suggested he would welcome the gesture.

She decided it would be best all round if she hurried proceedings along.

'How is Mrs O'Hagan?' Scarlet found it a relief to be able to sound genuinely sincere about something. 'Is she feeling better? She's not had a relapse or anything?'

'She is very much better, thank you, and I'm not contemplating any immediate legal action.'

'That's just as well because I've got no assets for you to strip.' You only had to look at the man to see his business tactics were every bit as unscrupulous as his rivals suggested.

A flicker of renewed interest appeared in Roman's deepset eyes. Now *that*, he decided, sounded much more like the girl he had spoken to on the phone.

'You take an interest in business? I got my MBA from Harvard; where did you get yours?'

'The London School of Economics,' she responded automatically.

Her reply might not have wiped the supercilious smirk off his face, but at least she had the pleasure of seeing him look mildly taken aback.

'You're trying to tell me that you've got a Masters in Business Administration?'

He had one of those perfectly straight patrician noses that

had been specifically designed to sneer down at lesser mortals. Scarlet would dearly have liked to punch it. Physical violence not being an option, she had to fall back on giving as good as she got in the sarcasm stakes.

'Actually I have, but it's not the sort of thing I'd normally drop into the conversation, because it might sound a bit pretentious.' She widened her eyes and adopted an expression of kittenish innocence. 'Don't you think?' she appealed to him. 'And,' she added thoughtfully, 'that sort of showing off might lead people to think I had a self-esteem issue.'

The stunned look in his eyes gave her a moment's intense, gleeful satisfaction.

'I doubt anyone is going to think you have a self-esteem issue,' Roman mused after a moment of startled, static silence. Whatever the hunched-shoulder stuff had been about, it had not been a confidence issue; her present manner made that obvious.

She inclined her head and smiled. 'Thank you,' she said, even though she was well aware his comment hadn't been meant as a compliment.

'Perhaps I didn't get this right. I thought you worked in the nursery?'

'I'm a nursery nurse,' she agreed with pride.

'Aren't you a little overqualified for the job?'

He stopped short of calling her a liar, but she could hear the amused scepticism in his voice. It was only by exerting superhuman restraint that Scarlet stopped herself supplying the names of referees who could confirm her qualifications and tell him how good she had been at her job.

'Actually I was under-qualified,' she explained calmly. 'I retrained. I was looking for job satisfaction.'

'Good for you!' he applauded with teeth-clenching insincerity. 'I've always said there's no shame in admitting you can't hack it.'

Scarlet's cheek muscles ached from maintaining a fixed smile. 'You have no idea how much I value your opinion.'

'I'm beginning to get a pretty good idea,' he returned drily. 'I believe you were very kind to my mother.'

'She's easy to be nice to; *she's* nice…' Scarlet literally bit her tongue to stop the flow of insults.

One perfectly symmetrical brow dark against his even-toned golden skin lifted to a politely interrogative angle.

'A very nice woman indeed,' Scarlet mumbled indistinctly.

She'd promised David—gosh, that seemed a lifetime ago now, not a few minutes—that she'd be on her best behaviour. Cutting the wretched man down to size was a self-indulgence she simply couldn't afford. It was also something she might not be capable of, she conceded.

Scarlet paused for a moment to consider her reckless behaviour objectively. The exercise gave rise to deep concern as she identified a worrying development, the adrenaline rush, the toe curling excitement she got from trading insults with him had a bizarrely addictive quality.

'She was full of praise for you.'

'She's kind; I hardly did anything,' she replied with suitable modesty, and for the second time that morning she had no argument. 'Not even call for an ambulance.' *You just couldn't leave well alone, could you, Scarlet?*

'Well, the best of us panic in a situation like that.'

'That's extremely understanding of you, but—'

'Yes, it is nice of me, isn't it? My assistant is worried I'll make you cry.'

'But,' she added, sending him a glare of simmering dislike, 'I *didn't* panic!' Scarlet announced, her chin lifting. '*Cry*…?' she added as his last comment sank in. 'I'm not going to cry!' she said, sounding insulted by the suggestion.

'I'm extremely relieved to hear it.' His dark head tilted a

little to one side as he examined her flushed, indignant face. 'So you think you made the right call, then, and you're prepared to defend your action, or rather lack of it?'

'Of course I didn't make the right call,' she surprised him by conceding with a grimace.

'But,' she added quickly, 'that wasn't because I panicked, it was because I took notice of—' She stopped abruptly, not wanting him to run away with the idea she was trying to pass the blame to someone else. 'Is this an official complaint? Because if it is I don't think you should be talking to me.'

'It isn't a complaint, official or otherwise, unless you particularly want it to be.'

Scarlet's jaw tightened at the blatant sarcasm in his voice. 'Then you came to apologise for being so rude to me?' she suggested innocently.

The hooded lids lowered in a lazy fashion but there was nothing remotely lazy about the spark in his eyes. *'Pushing it.'*

Scarlet conceded this lightest of warning with a shrug and rubbed the goose-bumps that had broken out over her forearms. When his voice dropped to a husky murmur that way it had an almost tactile quality.

She had the distinct impression that he wouldn't have minded it if she had ignored him. Roman O'Hagan was coming across as a man who enjoyed a fight and enjoyed winning even more. She could see why he didn't lose often, his dark eyes contained a gleam in them that suggested he had the intelligence to match his stunning looks.

The idea of pulverising him verbally was still an awfully attractive one, if deeply unrealistic.

'You made quite an impression on my mother…you and your little daughter…?' As this was just a matter of going through the motions there didn't seem to be any need to be overly subtle about introducing the child into the conversation, Roman thought.

'Son.'

'Right,' he drawled.

He couldn't have sounded less interested. It wouldn't take much effort to make it a little less obvious he was here under sufferance, Scarlet thought, pursing her lips indignantly. 'Sam,' she supplied.

Roman watched her face soften unconsciously as she said the kid's name and thought, *She isn't actually that bad-looking.* His long lashes lowered, half concealing his eyes as he considered her small heart-shaped face—good skin, nice hair; it was a shame about the glasses, and of course the bizarre sense of style.

But he wasn't here to organise a make-over, he reminded himself. He was here to convince his mother she didn't have any grandchildren running around the country.

'My mother was concerned her collapse might have alarmed…Sam.'

'He didn't take it personally.' Her attempt at levity didn't evoke any response. God, this was heavy going. He had two modes; silent and nastily sarcastic. Clearly scintillating conversational skills were not part of his attraction! But then she already knew that his attraction was much more basic.

Her bland smile became strained as she ran her tongue across her dry lips and swallowed to relieve the nervous occlusion tightening her throat. 'Tell her he's fine.' *Oh, God, please let this be over soon.*

Her hazel eyes flickered to her wrist-watch. Ten minutes to lunch time, one of the busiest times of the day in the nursery. She shifted her weight restively from one leg to the other and repressed a sigh as she lifted her head.

She flushed lightly as Roman O'Hagan angled his sable brows expressively.

'Sorry, I should be somewhere else,' she explained, trying hard to make it sound as if this were something she was sorry about.

'Am I boring you?' Women didn't make a habit of looking at their watches when they were in his company. 'Or should I have made an appointment?'

The sardonic note in his rich velvet voice brought the colour rushing back to her cheeks.

'Well, if I'd had a little warning I could have told you that today isn't very convenient,' Scarlet agreed bluntly. 'I realise,' she added, 'that my time isn't as valuable as yours…' It was the total shock she saw momentarily flicker in his eyes that halted the flow of indiscreet observations.

What's wrong with me? I told David I'd be nice to him. It's not like it requires any great skill, just an ability to keep my mouth shut. Getting herself out of this one was going to require some quick thinking, or talking at least.

'Which, of course, it isn't. I'm sure an hour of your time would cost me loads, whereas I only get paid…but I don't suppose you get paid by the hour. And I don't want an hour of it or even five minutes, though it's obviously been an enormous thrill to meet you.' Was that obsequious enough? She lifted a weary hand to her head. *Oh, God…! Do I sound as much of a blithering idiot as I feel?*

'I'm delighted you're thrilled.'

I might die of humiliation, she decided, listening to the amusement in his deep voice.

'And I'm sorry if this is inconvenient,' he continued, 'but the vice-chancellor said there would be no problem.'

'Well, he would, wouldn't he? You're influential and rich and…' Her scornful observation faded as their glances meshed once again. 'That is, you're…*sorry.*' She managed to force her lips into a stiff smile. 'That was rude.'

'Yes, it was.' It was hard to tell from his languid agreement if he was annoyed or amused.

David will kill me. She exhaled noisily and ran her hands, palm-flat, over her face in a brisk scrubbing motion.

'I get the impression you're having a bad day?'

'What makes you say that?' she asked gloomily.

A laugh was drawn from his beautifully tanned throat. Scarlet lifted her face, startled by the deeply attractive sound. He smiled at her, his teeth flashing very white in his dark face. She blinked—for a moment he had reminded her of Sam; the fleeting similarity made her almost feel disposed to think he might not be quite the monster she had imagined.

'Well, if you carry on like this on a regular basis I can't imagine they'd carry on paying you that *enormous* salary you spoke of.'

She let her hands fall away and shook her head. 'I earn every penny I make. Especially today.'

'What's happened to make this a bad day?'

'*You*…well, not just you,' she added with a self-condemnatory grimace. 'And I don't mean you personally, it's just I didn't like leaving the staff to struggle. I've been putting in lots of extra hours this week to cover for sickness.'

'And what happens if you get sick?'

'Oh, I never get sick.'

Her solemn conviction struck him as funny. She must have picked up on his amusement because she added defensively. 'I can't remember the last time I was ill.'

'Aren't you afraid of tempting fate?'

Scarlet suspected he was making fun of her. 'I'm not superstitious,' she told him her expression contemptuous.

'You've never pinched spilt salt over your shoulder, or counted magpies in a field, or crossed your fingers for luck?'

She shook her head. 'Of course not. Don't you believe me?'

'I think everyone's superstitious deep down; it's human nature.'

This point of view amazed her. '*You're* superstitious?' she asked incredulously.

'My father's Irish, my mother's Italian—the odds were stacked.' His broad shoulders lifted. 'What choice do I have?'

'Well, I'm not superstitious, but I am really glad that your mother is better.'

'But you've somewhere else you need to be,' he completed smoothly.

It would be overstating it to call the glint in his eyes annoyance, *but…*! She probably was making the fact she couldn't stick being in his company a bit obvious.

'That's very understanding of you, Mr O'Hagan.'

'Perhaps we could continue our discussion over lunch?'

Scarlet heard his voice through a faint buzz in her ears as she tried to contemplate what he'd just said.

'Lunch…?' she parroted vaguely.

Best to look on this as a reflex—her hormones had gone into primitive autopilot mode and were acting independently of her brain. Hence the weakness in her legs, the warm heat thrumming through her body and the painful spasms knotting her stomach. He was an attractive man, end of story, no need to complicate it further.

'Bring your son, by all means.'

'*Discussion?*' There seemed to be a time delay in her ability to translate what he was saying. 'We weren't having a discussion.' Her straight brows arranged themselves in an interrogative line. '*Lunch!*'

There's no such thing as a free lunch!

'*Good God, no!*'

His eyes widened fractionally, but other than that nothing in his manner revealed his reaction to her response. It wasn't that he was conceited, but a lifetime of being pursued and flattered by women had left Roman ill prepared to have an invitation of lunch rejected in an attitude of blatant revulsion.

'Well, I know where to come if I need my ego deflated.'

Belatedly Scarlet recalled her promise to David. She tried to soften her blunt reply.

'That is…it's very kind of you to offer,' she added, even though every instinct told her this was not a man predisposed to be kind.

She just stopped herself lifting her hand, which would have drawn attention to her face, which felt as though it were on fire. This was a man who never did anything without a reason. Which left the question, why had he asked her to lunch? Did he have some elaborate punishment in mind because she had answered back to him on the phone?

'Like I said the flu epidemic has left us very short-staffed today.'

'But otherwise you'd have been delighted to come?'

In face of this sardonic observation it took all of Scarlet's will-power to conceal her feelings behind a blank expression.

What were her feelings? In one word—shallow; this was biology at its most basic. She knew what lust felt like, and never had it been less welcome or so extreme, but when you came right down to it she really shouldn't have been letting it get to her this way. There was absolutely no need to stress; it wasn't as if she'd never felt sexual attraction before. She knew about the tightening in her stomach and the rest; it was a biological response—like sneezing.

She took a deep breath and was conscious of the fabric of her borrowed top chafing against her erect nipples; lower, the tell-tale liquid heat was even more of a give-away. *Sneezing?* Maybe not the best analogy.

She saw a smile touch his sensual lips. To her horrified eyes it held a knowing quality that suggested she wasn't hiding anything from him; she felt a flare of anger—her condition was entirely his doing.

'If you'll excuse me, I have to go,' she told him abruptly.

'Rain check?'

She looked at him blankly. If he thought she was strange and peculiar, that was fine, because she was. Being attracted, even in a blind, mindless way, to a man like this could quite safely be categorised as peculiar…also wantonly stupid and brainless!

'Fine, whatever…' she mumbled, before virtually throwing herself through the door in her haste to remove herself from the room.

She literally bumped into David about thirty seconds after she had emerged from his office. She suspected he had been lurking there waiting for her to appear.

'Steady, you're in a hurry,' he said, placing his hands on her shoulders to steady her. 'You came around that corner like you had the hounds of hell on your heels.'

After what she had just endured the hounds of hell would be child's play.

'The girls will be missing me. I promised I'd be back to help with the lunches.'

David's right hand remained on her shoulder. 'How did it go?'

'What…? Oh, with Mr O'Hagan? Fine, absolutely fine.'

David looked at her face and groaned. 'Oh, God, you're such a terrible liar, you always were. What did you do?'

'I didn't *do* anything.'

'But you said something.'

Scarlet's expression grew defensive. 'Of course I said something. I may not warm to womanising playboys—' annoyingly this was something that was hard to say without sounding, not only prejudiced, but distressingly intolerant '—but I'm not a total idiot.' Actually the jury was still out on that one.

'Well, this particular womanising playboy finds time in his schedule to run a highly successful international company.' He looked into her stubborn face and sighed. 'Would it hurt you to be nice to the man, Scarlet?'

'How nice would that be? Will treating everything he says as a pearl of wisdom do, or did you want me to sleep with him?'

'Do you have to be facetious, Scarlet?' David demanded, allowing his aggravation with her to surface.

'It's easier than—'

'Easier than what, Scarlet?'

Good question. 'He's not an easy man.'

'I found him perfectly affable, but, easy or not, Scarlet, he is funding a number of bursaries to help students from less-well-off backgrounds.'

The seconds ticked by while Scarlet stood staring at him with her mouth slightly ajar. Finally she gulped and took a deep breath.

'You're kidding!' Her grin faded as no corresponding smile appeared on David's face. 'Oh, God, I feel such a...'

'Narrow-minded, judgemental?'

'Amongst other things,' she admitted miserably.

David shook his head. 'I don't know why you have a problem accepting the man is capable of acting altruistically?'

Scarlet did. It wasn't the man; it was the type of person he represented.

She had no problem seeing past an unattractive face, and

she didn't judge anyone by their accent, their bank balance or the car they drove, but when it came to people who lived their lives being seen in the right places wearing the right clothes and with the right people she came over with terminal intolerance. She knew it and wasn't proud of it, but she couldn't help it.

Scarlet knew about people like that. Her sister had been a member of their very exclusive club, and how many of them had visited when Abby had been ill in hospital, losing her hair after intensive chemo? Abby's friends had had more important things to do, when she had contacted the names in her sister's address book and explained the situation and told them how much it would cheer her sister up to see a friendly face.

A few had made vague promises, but in the end not a single one of those *good friends* had turned up to show support, she recalled bitterly. When the going got tough, the Roman O'Hagans of this world disappeared in their fast cars.

'I'm not kidding. This is not common knowledge,' David added, laying a warning finger to his lips and looking as though he was regretting sharing the confidential information with her. 'Mr O'Hagan was most insistent on his name not being made public.' David gave a wry smile as he thought of all the name plaques he had unveiled in his career. 'Which makes him unique in my experience,'

'Really!' she exclaimed, unable to stop the bitchy retort. 'I'd have thought he'd be used to it! Well, he's not exactly publicity shy, is he?' she added defensively. It seemed pretty perverse to Scarlet that someone who lived his life in the glare of publicity would be bothered about his altruism being made public. 'Maybe it's a tax thing?'

She realised that, far from agreeing with her, David was looking annoyed, and added with as much conviction as she could muster, 'Or maybe he's a very modest, generous man.'

CHAPTER FIVE

SCARLET lowered the blinds over the glass partition and removed her borrowed finery before folding it neatly over the back of her chair. Standing there in just her white cotton pants, she shook out her own clean clothes. Creased, certainly, but a whole lot better than what she had been wearing.

If she had looked half decent would she have emerged from her encounter with Roman O'Hagan looking less of a loon?

Such speculation was pointless. Scarlet turned her thoughts firmly away from that traumatic and humiliating interview she had just endured—she never had been a big fan of post-mortems—and pulled her cream slim-cut pedal pushers over her bottom and slid the zip home over her narrow, some might say boyish, hips.

She took her tee shirt between her hands and attempted to stretch it this way and that without much success. A size six now, but it had survived the hot washing cycle in the industrial-sized machine a local firm had kindly donated to them better than her bra, which had come out looking like a dish rag.

She heard the knock on the door just as she was pulling her tee shirt over her head.

'Come in, Angie,' she called out, her voice muffled. 'I just wanted to ask if you'd mind covering for Barbara in the morning.'

Roman, preceded by his entrance card, a giant teddy bear, pushed the slightly ajar door fully open and walked in.

His experience of buying gifts for small children was limited, but he knew enough to know that the case of excellent claret he had put down for his godson on the occasion of his christening and the additions he had generously donated to the child's investment portfolio at Christmas and birthdays would not be suitable on this occasion. Wine and shares being inappropriate gifts he had sought the advice of his PA.

'What sort of gift is appropriate for a child of three?'

'Boy or girl?'

'Boy.'

'How much money do you want to spend?'

'I don't want to be seen as throwing money at the problem.'

'Right, but you do want to be seen as thoughtful; that's always more difficult.'

'Do you like your job?'

Alice grinned. 'All children like teddy bears, Roman,' she told him confidently. 'Yeah, a teddy bear is a good bet. A big one.'

He had followed her advice with some misgivings. Alice's knowledge of fitness videos, football and chocolate was second to none, but she had never struck him as being particularly child-orientated, unless you counted his kid brother, Luca, but you never could tell with women. Some of the most unlikely ones, women who had publicly declared themselves wedded to their careers, one day started looking on you as potential father material.

He had learnt to read the signals. When he became a father he wanted it to be *his* decision.

Roman was perfectly aware of his responsibility to provide an heir and perpetuate the family name…as if the world didn't have enough O'Hagans in it. But just in case it slipped his mind, his father, who seemed to think his eldest son might well walk under a moving bus at any moment, obligingly reminded him of the fact at regular intervals.

He would get round to doing what his father wanted in his own time, but at the moment he didn't have a son, he'd never met this woman before today, and this was a pointless exercise. There were a hundred other things that he could and should be doing.

Despite these facts he was determined to see the farce through to the end, because he always completed tasks he began. But more importantly, this way, when his mother asked, as she would, he would be able to tell her with a clear conscience that he had seen mother and child and they were nothing to do with him.

Nothing less was going to satisfy her.

Also in the short space of time that had elapsed since Scarlet Smith had knocked back his lunch invitation, Roman had totally forgotten that, not only had he regretted issuing the invite the moment he'd made it—did he even know any restaurants where they served dribbling toddlers?—but he had also lost track of the crucial fact that he hadn't issued the spur-of-the-moment invitation out of any desire for her abrasive company, but because he couldn't think of an easier way of getting to see her son.

'I'd be really grateful,' Scarlet said, still thinking she was talking to Angie. She grunted as she groped to insert her hand through the arm hole. 'Hold on a mo, I think this thing has shrunk.'

She clicked her tongue in regret. The tee shirt had been produced at their last fundraising event and it was decorated with self-portraits produced by the older children, including Sam. Now it was shrunk it would be lovingly stored with the growing collection of childhood memorabilia she was accumulating.

'It could have been worse, the machine totally shredded

my bra,' she confided. 'Not that I'm in any position to complain. This is one of those times being flat-chested pays off,' she huffed with a strangulated laugh as she inhaled deeply to allow the over-stretched fabric to cover and compress her small, pointed breasts.

Roman wasn't complaining either; he had no objections to 'holding on a mo.' Beneath the enticing expanse of slender back he had an excellent opportunity to appreciate the curvy shape and firmness of a small but perfectly formed bottom complete with strategically placed dimple above her peachy left buttock. And he didn't think she was flat chested; his entrance into the room had been perfectly timed to coincide with the brief bare-breasted interval.

He'd been taken unawares; the sight of pink-tipped, delightfully bouncy breasts had frozen him to the spot and primitive urges oblivious to the social restraints of being a modern man had surged into painful life.

It was extraordinary but, far from being shapeless, Scarlet Smith had an enticing body, slim with supple, succulent and very sexy curves. The transformation was nothing short of mind-blowing.

That made it official. He did not have a son—no way would he have forgotten sleeping with Scarlet Smith!

Smoothing the slightly creased cotton fabric over her flat midriff, Scarlet turned around. The smile on her face faded as she saw who was standing there. 'You!' she gasped accusingly.

For a horror-struck moment, she peered up at Roman before her brain got back into gear. She forced herself to release the breath painfully trapped in her chest, unfolded her arms, which she'd wrapped across her bosom in an instinctively protective gesture, and groped behind her on the desk for the glasses she'd set aside a few moments earlier.

'Dio! It's absolutely amazing.'

It took her several seconds for her slightly unsteady hands to locate her glasses from the table where she had put them. She slid them back onto her nose and his dark, fatally handsome face slipped into focus.

She was tempted to take them off again.

Roman frowned. Before she had replaced the glasses he had seen a red welt across the bridge of her nose, livid against the pallor of her skin. It was obviously caused by those stupid glasses. It was a crime to hide such beautiful eyes behind thick lenses. Didn't she know glasses were meant to be fashion accessories? That you could get paper-thin lenses and attractive frames these days.

'Those spectacles are too big and heavy for your face,' he censured in a gruff, distracted voice.

Scarlet shook her head ruefully. 'I know, but five years ago they were the height of fashion.' She gave a wry grin. 'It was my funky period,' she explained drily. 'I can't wait to put them back in the dark, dusty drawer they were hiding in,' she confessed.

'Then why don't you?'

'They won't let me wear my lenses until my corneal abrasion heals, and it hardly seemed worth forking out for a new pair.'

'*Corneal abrasion!* You injured your eyes?'

'The right one.' She lifted her hand towards her right eye, which showed no visible signs of the injury she spoke of. 'A freak accident—amusing really. A baby hit me in the face with a rattle, would you believe?'

Most people thought it amusing when she explained the circumstances, but not Roman O'Hagan, it seemed. His lips thinned in disapproval and his nostrils flared.

'This *amusing* accident could have cost you your eyesight.'

Her expression reflected her opinion of his bizarre pursuit of the subject. 'Well, I wouldn't go *that* far…'

'That much I can see.' The grim condemnatory note in his voice seemed a bit over the top to Scarlet. 'I suppose you'd have an equally offhand attitude to walking across the road without looking? You only have one set of eyes; it's generally a good idea to look after them,' he reproached sternly.

To hear him talk you'd think I did it deliberately, Scarlet thought.

'I'm as fond of my eyes as the next person.'

'I'm sure a great many people are fond of your eyes—they are beautiful. As is the rest of you.'

Beautiful eyes—? Beautiful rest of me? Before Scarlet had time to properly assimilate this extraordinary information, she saw where his own hot eyes had come to rest, and her arms reassumed their protective position. She breathed deeply as her entire body was engulfed in a wave of mortified heat that to her mind was worryingly out of proportion with the situation.

If he had shown any inclination to say something more on the subject she doubted she would have heard it past the clamour of her hammering heartbeat. Only he didn't show any inclination to speak…he wasn't showing any inclination to do anything beyond look at her in a way that made her go literally weak at the knees.

'Dear God,' she snapped. 'Anyone would think you'd never seen a woman without her shirt on before!'

And from the way you're acting, the voice in her head added snidely, *you'd think you'd never been looked at by a man before.*

It was true, his smouldering stare was making Scarlet's erect nipples pinch hard and burn. It was deeply mortifying that she had no control whatsoever over what was happening to her.

Roman gave a cough of laughter as dark eyes returned to her face. 'Sorry, I wasn't expecting to find you half dressed.' As he spoke his glance slid once more over her slender figure, and his chest lifted as a deep sigh vibrated through his lean, powerful frame.

'My God,' he observed, shaking his head. 'You look different…different in a good way, in case I didn't make myself clear.' Actually Roman doubted he had ever been less articulate in his life. 'I didn't mean to embarrass you.'

'Strange, I got the impression you were quite enjoying embarrassing me.'

One corner of his mouth lifted in appreciation of her comment. 'Do you play chess?'

'*Pardon?*' she said, sure she must have misheard him.

'Do you play chess?' he repeated.

Warily she nodded, still unsure of where this was going.

Roman's eyes narrowed. 'You either win with style or lose dramatically—?'

This accurate assessment stunned her. 'How could you know that?'

'You're reckless, and you rely on inspiration. Playing an unpredictable partner is always exciting,' he observed. 'Perhaps we could play some time…?'

Play with Roman O'Hagan?

Before she had time to respond to this proposal he added casually, 'And if you're wondering what I saw when I walked in—I didn't see a thing.'

Scarlet was now ninety per cent sure he was lying, which was no comfort to her. If he managed to unsettle his business rivals with this sort of thoroughness, no wonder they talked about him in financial circles as though he were the second coming.

Her chin lifted to a bolshy angle. 'I'm not the slightest bit embarrassed.' *Now that, Scarlet, is really going to convince him.*

'Why should you be? We're both adults…*consenting* adults.'

The throaty 'consenting' sent a secret shiver down her spine. 'I just wasn't expecting to see you standing there.' Despite her best efforts, she was unable to keep the accusatory note from her voice as she added, 'You surprised me.'

Understatement.

If another man, say Jimmy from the post room had walked in and caught her in the middle of getting changed, if she had inadvertently discussed her bra with him she would not exactly have fallen apart. She would have seen the funny side of the situation.

Right now she didn't feel like laughing.

She watched as he shook his head as if to clear his thoughts and released his breath in a soft sibilant hiss.

'If it's any comfort I got a shock too.' Now was not the perfect occasion, but a man couldn't choose when he was going to be overwhelmed by lust.

'I thought you were someone else…a colleague,' she added.

'Shall I go out and come back in again?' he offered.

'Don't be silly,' she snapped. 'Is there something I can do for you?'

Roman scrutinised her warm face thoughtfully for a moment before crossing the room.

Scarlet watched as he sat the ludicrously large teddy bear he was carrying in her chair behind the desk. She looked at it. It wasn't the sort of item that you could miss, but her attention had been so focused on the man himself she hadn't even noticed he was carrying anything until that moment.

She doubted if she would have noticed if he had arrived accompanied by a full male voice choir!

His burden disposed of, Roman looked at Scarlet once more. He ran a hand through his glossy thatch of sleek dark hair. The action, like everything he did, was rivetingly graceful.

'Is this about our telephone conversation yesterday?' he asked.

'I don't know what you mean.'

'I seem to bother you.'

If he knew how much she would have died of sheer mortification. 'I'm assuming you came here for a reason, Mr O'Hagan.'

'Or can you simply not bear to be in the same room as me?'

'I don't want to be rude, Mr O'Hagan, but I'm really in a hurry. You were horrible,' she admitted, despite her previous decision not to refer to the incident, 'but no more than I expected from someone like you.'

'Ouch...!' But beyond threatening to sue you, have I done something to upset you?' he wondered, a curious frown deepening the lines above the bridge of his masterful nose.

Other than undress me mentally? Not that she imagined for one moment that she had received any special treatment. Roman obviously had a very Latin attitude when it came to ogling women. Especially if they were wearing tight tee shirts and no bra!

'Of course not.' Even she was unconvinced by her tone. 'Now, if you could tell me what I can do to help you? But I really do need to crack on.'

He ignored her interruption totally. 'I didn't really see how I could have offended you given we've not met before—though,' he added, pausing to allow his eyes to traverse the slim, shapely length of her body, 'maybe we have when you were wearing another disguise. I must say I prefer this one.'

She despised his slick patter and the fact it made her heartbeat accelerate.

'Oh, that.' She laughed uneasily, partly because his un-inhibited scrutiny of her body was not something she was comfortable with. She was even less comfortable with her body's response to that scrutiny. A shivery sensation slipped down her spine and she experienced a moment's blinding panic.

Some people became withdrawn when they were nervous. Scarlet talked.

'One of the children threw up all over me this morning—projectile.' *And he really wants to know this.* 'I usually keep some spare stuff here, but it's always the way—the one time you need them they're not here. The girls rallied around and lent me some clothes until mine could be cleaned. Though we do keep a box of spare clothes, for them, the children, obviously, just not for me.' The hearty laugh she heard emerge from her lips sounded just as unbalanced as the babble that had preceded it.

Scarlet closed her eyes. If Roman O'Hagan hadn't lost the will to live after that, she had. The room was filled with the sound of her own laboured breathing.

'I would say that constitutes a bad day.'

The quiver of laughter she heard in his deep voice brought her head up. Hazel eyes shining with indignation through the lenses of her glasses, she glared at him. 'It's not funny.'

'But not a tragedy either.'

'Are you suggesting I can't laugh at myself?' she demanded indignantly. 'Because, let me tell you, I have a *great* sense of humour...' she met his wry eyes and added with a defensive sniff '...normally.'

She didn't know why she was acting like this. She wasn't a naturally aggressive person; her temper was even; she was one of life's natural conciliators. There was just something about this man that brought out a latent combative streak in her nature.

'Is there something I can do to help you…?' she repeated.

He gestured towards the bear sitting in her chair. 'I had left it in my car. My mother thought your son might like it.'

'That's very kind of her.'

'Perhaps I could give it to him?'

She tried, but couldn't come up with a legitimate reason to refuse this casual request. 'He's in the play room. I'll show you the way,' she offered, only partially managing to mask her extreme reluctance to do so.

Halfway through the door she backtracked and pulled her denim jacket off the hook behind the door. 'It's chilly,' she told him, shrugging it on.

CHAPTER SIX

THE play room, normally a scene of organised chaos, was unusually peaceful when they entered. The younger children were sitting on the floor listening raptly to Angie tell a story.

Angie paused when they entered, her eyes widening a little when she identified the man beside Scarlet.

'Children,' she said, rising to her feet, 'we have a visitor.'

Royalty could not have produced more awe in her voice, Scarlet thought cynically.

'Roman O'Hagan.' Roman, his smile all charm, extended his hand to Angie who accepted it with an eagerness that to Scarlet's critical eye was *too* eager, fawning even, she concluded, viewing the older woman's response to their visitor with a jaundiced eye.

'Oh, I know who you are,' Angie replied with a grin. 'It was only yesterday we were looking at photos of you at that film première in Scarlet's magazine.'

Thank you for that, Angie, now he thinks I'm a secret groupie. 'Were we? I don't remember.'

Roman angled her a speculative look and she glared back at him aggressively.

'Sure you do, you put the magazine in your drawer, Scarlet.'

'For the recipe section—I'm going to make the risotto.' There was a layer of frost on Scarlet's words, which Angie seemed totally oblivious to.

'Isn't that a bit ambitious for you? Scarlet can't cook,' she added in a confidential aside to Roman. 'But she can eat for England and never put on an ounce. Me, I put on a

62

pound if I so much as look at a grain of rice.' She shook her head at the injustice of it.

'There's nothing wrong with womanly curves.'

'That's what my Bob says.'

Scarlet, who couldn't believe that any woman could fall for such a corny line, stared at her friend—her old-enough-to-know-better friend—who was visibly preening.

Roman, head tilted to one side, considered the older woman, a smile playing about his fascinating mouth. 'Is that a Donegal accent I'm hearing?'

Angie laughed. 'Not many people here can tell the difference.'

Without any apparent effort, he slipped into a wildly attractive soft brogue. 'I'm a Kerry man myself, on my da's side anyhow.'

'I have to tell you, Mr O'Hagan,' Angie gushed, 'those photos in Scarlet's magazine didn't do you justice.' She turned to her friend for support. 'Did they, Scarlet?'

'Angie, I think it might be an idea if you got back to the story.' Scarlet gave a significant nod towards the children. They were growing restive.

God bless restive children.

To her immense relief the distraction worked.

'Timothy Jones, don't pull Bethany's hair!' Angie exclaimed, wading in to calmly separate two small figures.

'She pulled mine.'

'Angie, if I could just see Sam for a minute.'

'Sure thing, you go with your mum, Sam. Now, children, say goodbye to Mr O'Hagan and thank him for this lovely present. My, isn't he just gorgeous?' she exclaimed.

Scarlet was pretty certain she wasn't talking about the stuffed toy; she certainly wasn't looking at it.

Roman had a choice; he could tell the eager faces that

the toy wasn't for them or he could hand it over. He handed it over.

Scarlet hid a smile as she tucked Sam's hand in her own. 'Don't worry, Sam knows about sharing, don't you, sweetheart?'

Sam, who was looking with saucer-like eyes up at the tall man standing beside his mother, didn't reply.

'However, he doesn't always like it,' she admitted drily. 'Say hello to Mr O'Hagan, Sam. He's not normally so tongue-tied,' she added, bending down to speak in her son's ear. 'Say hello to Mr O'Hagan, darling.'

'Hello,' Sam grunted, looking at his toes.

Scarlet gave an affectionate sigh and ruffled his dark hair before standing up.

'Hello there, Sam.'

Scarlet happened to be looking at Roman O'Hagan at the moment Sam lifted his head—*so nothing unusual there*— but what she saw was unusual. Unusual and inexplicable. At least as far as she could see there was no immediately obvious reason why the colour would seep out of Roman's face until his vibrant golden skin looked like marble. He stilled, the nerve that throbbed in the hollow of his lean cheek about the only movement in his body. There was no evidence that he was breathing until a deep, soundless sigh shuddered through his body, lifting his ribcage.

As she watched he dropped casually down on his haunches. 'Hello, Sam. I'm Roman.'

He sounded so normal and his whole body language was so relaxed that Scarlet wondered if she had imagined what had gone before.

'Do you like teddy bears, Sam?' Roman ran his hand over the little boy's dark head.

'They're *all right,* but I'm a big boy—I prefer footballs.'

'I'll remember that,' Roman promised.

'I'm going to be a footballer when I grow up.'

Roman made the appropriate impressed noises.

'Are you Mummy's friend?' she was deeply embarrassed to hear Sam ask.

Roman lifted his head; his eyes, which considering his manner with the child had been so relaxed and friendly, were bewilderingly cold. The hostility emanating from his lean body was equally pointed.

He turned back to the boy.

'I'm going to be, Sam, so we'll be seeing each other a lot,' he promised with a smile before he straightened up.

Scarlet held in her indignation until they got out to the corridor.

'Why on earth did you say that to Sam?' she demanded, turning on him angrily. 'He may only be three, but he remembers things.'

'Good. He won't be surprised the next time he sees me.'

'He won't be seeing you and neither will I. To be blunt, Mr O'Hagan, I don't actually like you very much.'

'Actually, Miss Smith, I'm not wild about you either…but I think you'll find you'll be seeing a lot more of me.'

Scarlet stared after him with a baffled expression as he retreated. To say his behaviour was bizarre would have been an understatement.

Still, one thing was certain: if she had anything to do with it neither she nor Sam would be seeing him again, despite his odd claim to the contrary!

CHAPTER SEVEN

SAM was spending Friday night at his best friend Thomas's house. This was the second time he had had a sleep-over. The first time Scarlet had spent the entire night worrying and hanging around the phone just in case an emergency had arisen that necessitated her rushing out of the house.

She had even mentally worked out the quickest routes to the two local hospitals, working on the assumption you couldn't be *too* prepared and it was always better to assume the worst.

The telephone hadn't rung and, far from crying for her, Sam had had a great time. The reciprocal sleep-over had gone equally well.

This time Scarlet was determined not to go weird again; she was not going to let the over-anxious mum thing turn her into a basket case. Instead she was going to look on this as an opportunity to enjoy a few self-indulgent hours alone. She would relax if it killed her! she determined grimly.

Her plans included a long, luxurious soak in a hot bath of decadent bubbles and using the moisturising face mask that guaranteed to bring the youthful bloom back to tired skin. After that there were a box of chocolates and a feel-good video with her name on them.

The opening credits of *It's a Wonderful Life* had just finished when the doorbell rang. She had forgotten that plans were an invitation for things to go wrong, especially when that plan was an evening of unadulterated indulgence.

'Damn!' she swore as she paused the film, hitched up the legs of her slightly too long pyjama bottoms and slid her feet into her slippers. 'Hold your horses,' she muttered crossly under her breath as she trudged to the door.

If Sam had been home she would have been a lot crankier; the chance of him sleeping through the racket their caller was making was just about nil. The doorbell was so insistent that she almost missed the sound of the phone ringing as she passed by.

Scarlet dived for it.

Her heart thudding with trepidation, she lifted it to her ear. *I knew the sleep-over was a daft idea. Three is much too young to be encouraging independence in a child...a child of three should be home with his mother.*

By the time she had politely heard out the person on the line selling double glazing, her heart rate had almost returned to normal and the person ringing the doorbell had begun to hammer on the door with their fist.

It was a very angry sound.

Though not always as security conscious as she might be Scarlet had no problem remembering in this instance to leave the safety chain on as she opened the door a crack. Of all the people she had imagined to discover standing there, Roman O'Hagan had not even featured on the list.

Her exclamation of, 'Gracious!' hardly covered her feelings as she peered up at the tall, commanding figure standing in the hallway.

She swallowed convulsively as her pulse rate shot off the scale. The fluttering sensation low in her belly combined with the difficulty she had breathing made it hard for her to do anything but gape. He was worth gaping at. Gosh, but he looked good, and my, she thought, attempting to nudge her appreciation towards the safer direction of scorn, didn't he know it?

He removed the designer shades he wore and tucked them into the breast pocket of his jacket. The dark, wintry eyes that surveyed her coldly were even less reassuring than the mirrored lenses had been!

It had been ten days since she'd last seen him... *I was counting?* He could not have altered since then, but the hard angles on his face did seem more defined this evening, as though he might have lost weight. But his greyhound-lean frame had not carried any excess flesh the last time. Perhaps it was the black leather jacket and tailored dark trousers that hugged the muscular contours of his long thighs that made him look longer and leaner and just generally harder.

If he'd been auditioning for the part of a dangerous but fatally attractive gangster he'd have got the job on the spot! The sprinkling of designer stubble across his jaw and hollow cheeks only intensified the aura of menace that hung around his sinfully gorgeous person.

The discovery that it was hard to maintain your anger with someone who was blinking innocently up at you did not improve Roman's mood. His jaw clenched because he knew that under baggy pyjamas and the glowing, baby smooth contours of her make-up-free face there lurked a woman who was living a lie.

Even if she didn't know he was the boy's father, she sure as hell knew she wasn't the mother! Besides, what was it his mother had said?

'Ignorance is no defence' Scarlet Smith—if that was her name?—was about to find out it was no defence in his eyes either.

His son was growing up without a father—that wasn't something that had happened by accident. Oh, yes, there were a lot of questions he wanted answered.

Scarlet Smith was going to do the answering.

For all he knew, everything about her was a lie. The curly knot scrunched casually on the top of her head, which made her look simultaneously vulnerable and sexy, was probably contrived to do just that.

'What the hell kept you?' he growled. 'Open the door.'

'I was on the phone.' Scarlet's beleaguered brain having finally accepted the fact that it was actually Roman standing out in the hallway and not some hallucination, she began to move on to other stuff, such as what was he doing here? 'What are you…how…?' She stopped, the blood draining from her face as a possible explanation presented itself to her.

'The Bradleys sent you.' Her worst fears were realised when he didn't deny it.

The Bradleys were exactly the sort of people he *would* know.

Tom was something important in films and Nancy, who wore floaty clothes and cooked like an angel, wrote a foodie newspaper column in a national newspaper; in short the sort of female that left Scarlet feeling sadly inadequate. They lived in a fantastic house, employed an au pair and a gardener, and most likely had dinner guests like Roman.

Her imagination went into overdrive. Oh, my God, it was so bad they hadn't been able to break the news over the phone.

'What's happened to Sam? You can tell me,' she added, an icy calm settling over her as she prepared herself to hear the worst.

Roman's dark eyes scanned her distressed features; the only trace of colour in her face was supplied by her jewel-bright eyes. He appeared about to say something and then changed his mind.

'Just tell me,' she begged. Imagining was so bad, could the reality be worse?

'Let me in.'

'Of course, of course,' she cried, fumbling with the door

chain, her hands trembling. 'Have they taken him to the hospital?' She pushed her fingers into her hair, dislodging one of her hair grips; a section of hair slithered free, falling across her cheek as she flung the door wide and stepped aside for him to enter.

Think, Scarlet, think... 'Now let me think...' she said out loud as she tried to organise her thoughts and keep panic at arm's length. 'Yes, get dressed.' She flashed him a white-faced but encouraging smile. 'It won't take me a minute to get dressed,' she promised, turning to suit her words to action.

Roman closed the front door. 'I don't know who the Bradleys are.'

Halfway to the bedroom door, Scarlet stopped. *'What?'*

'I don't know the Bradleys and, as far as I am aware, Sam is not in hospital.'

Her marble-pale brow creased. 'But you said...'

'No, actually, I didn't, you said.'

She started shaking in reaction as a massive wave of relief hit her. Impetuously she wrapped her arms around him and hugged hard. 'Thank God!' she breathed fervently.

Roman looked at the heart-shaped face complete with misty eyes and trusting sunny smile tilted up to him and felt his focus slipping. He'd come here to uncover some truths, not fantasise about a sexy mouth and what he'd like to do with it.

It wasn't until she encountered his broodingly black and icy cold mesmeric eyes that Scarlet recalled with a rush of scalding embarrassment that she wasn't dealing with someone into spontaneous hugs. Feeling a total idiot, she unpeeled herself from him and stepped away with a self-conscious grimace and a murmur of, 'Sorry.'

She tucked her hands behind her back and resisted the self-indulgent impulse to smooth down the non-existent creases in his jacket, recognizing that the impulse to touch his lithe body no longer had anything to do with spontaneity and a hell of a lot to do with sexual curiosity. It was deeply mortifying to have to acknowledge she had enjoyed the contact with a very well-developed male physique.

She felt she had to offer some sort of explanation for her strange behaviour.

'I know he's perfectly safe with the Bradleys, but when I saw you I thought the worst…' She released a small self-derisive chuckle. 'But I expect you've already gathered that much.'

Her brow wrinkled as an inconsistency she had been too panic stricken to notice earlier struck her.

'Why didn't you say straight off that you didn't know the Bradleys?'

It wasn't as if he could have missed the fact she had been two steps away from hysteria.

'I wanted to talk to you and I wasn't sure you'd let me in.'

Scarlet stared at him. Staggeringly there was no *hint* of apology in his manner. His behaviour was so extraordinary that it took her a while to get her head around what he had done. 'You wanted to come in,' she repeated in a dangerously flat tone as her temper fizzed dramatically into life. 'You wanted to come in.'

Only someone totally callous could act with such calculated cruelty.

'I need to talk to you.'

'Oh, that makes it all right, then!' she said contemptuously.

His classically pure jawline tautened as a dark line appeared across his cheekbones. 'Will you calm yourself, woman?'

'I'm not a woman…well, not your woman, anyhow, and

for that,' she added with incoherent fervour, 'I shall be eternally grateful. *Nothing* makes it all right for you to scare me half to death that way. It was a totally *despicable* thing to do!'

And it also proved her first impressions had been right; he was a man who didn't care about anything but getting what he wanted! If other people got hurt in the process, so what? It didn't matter to Roman.

'You disgust me!' Her voice rose a quivering octave. 'Get out, get out of my home right now!'

'I think you're overreacting just a little here.'

Her eyes flashed pure green fire as she glared up at him. '*Overreacting?* I thought that Sam was—' She broke off, her voice suspended by tears as the nightmare images crowded into her head. 'Maybe I am overreacting,' she conceded huskily. 'But this is only the second time Sam has spent a night away from home and...' She shook her head. 'If you had a child maybe you'd understand.'

His nostrils flared and something she couldn't identify flashed in his eyes. 'I wanted to talk to you.'

From his expression she couldn't imagine he wanted to say anything nice.

'I realise that I should be thanking my lucky stars, but strangely I'm not.' She strode to the door and pulled it open. 'I don't want to talk to you, Mr O'Hagan, and you were right, I wouldn't have let you in.'

Why would she? To allow someone who was broadcasting dangerous and volatile into your home was asking for trouble. Every inch of his powerful frame suggested he was struggling to contain his anger and with limited success.

'If this has something to do with the university you should be speaking to David.'

His dark brows arched. '*University?*' he repeated, his lip

curling. 'You're a nursery nurse. Why would I come here if I wanted to discuss anything involving the university.'

'Frankly, I don't know,' she admitted. 'But it makes about as much sense as anything else I could come up with to explain you being here.'

And it was a lot more feasible than the inspired, but seriously misguided notion that Scarlet was embarrassed to admit she had entertained for a brief mad moment when she had seen him standing there. The one that relied on him having spent the last ten days wrestling with an overpowering attraction for her he could no longer resist.

So it wasn't exactly plausible, but it was a well-known fact that some men liked glasses and flat chests, and if you were going to fantasise you might as well do it properly.

He walked towards her and for a moment Scarlet thought he was going to carry on past her and through the door, but her optimism proved premature. Instead of walking through the door he casually wrenched it from her grasp. It closed with a very decisive click.

'I'm sorry if I alarmed you.' He watched her rub her shoulder and the indentation between his brows deepened. 'Did I hurt you?'

She looked from the closed door to the man—he was alarming her some more and also, much more disturbingly, he was exciting her. 'And that would bother you?' She delivered a brittle laugh. 'Credit me with a little intelligence.' *Even if I've shown precious little of it to date.* 'You obviously get a kick out of bullying women. And you're *not* sorry, so don't say you are,' she hissed furiously.

His eyes narrowed on her belligerent face. 'You make it extremely difficult for a man to be sorry,' he ground out grimly.

'Yes, I know you don't like me, which makes it even more difficult to imagine why you'd want to talk to me or what you'd want to say, and quite frankly I don't want to know!' she lied grandly as she opened the door again. 'Now, if you don't mind, it's late and I'm busy.'

His even teeth flashed white in his dark face as a smile that had nothing whatsoever to do with humour formed on his sensual lips. 'You won't sleep tonight…'

Scarlet froze, her body stiffening as if in anticipation of a blow.

'Curiosity killed the cat and you're going to be wondering what I did it for,' he warned. 'Admit it, you will.'

Scarlet exhaled. She was light-headed with relief and willing to admit almost anything. For a split second she had jumped to the totally irrational conclusion that he possessed some insider knowledge of the dreams that had given her several nights of broken sleep recently.

Dark, erotic dreams.

Angie is always telling me I need to get out more—she's right!

Was it possible that at some subconscious level she was as frustrated as her friend claimed? That could account for the dreams and the fact she hadn't been able to get him out of her head.

'I've told you, I'm busy,' she repeated dismissively.

'Well, you can tell him to clear off.' His fine nostrils quivered in distaste. 'I will not be dismissed.'

He might not know much about bringing up a child, but even he knew that a single mother with a series of boyfriends hardly provided the sort of stable background a child needed—*his* child needed.

She blinked, and tore her eyes from the nerve clenching spasmodically in the hollow of his lean cheek. This conversation was like walking in halfway through a film after the vital scene when the hero's motivations had been explained.

Roman would be the hero, of course; he had hero written all over him. She, on the other hand, would be one of the character actors, which would suit her—nobody remembered your name and you were always in work.

Fame was not something she craved.

Roman O'Hagan's touch, however, was; you had to face your weaknesses if you were going to overcome them.

'Him who?' she enquired, still without the faintest idea what he was getting at.

He swallowed, the action causing the muscles in his brown throat to visibly ripple, and gave her a look of simmering hostility.

Scarlet heard a door in the hallway outside open and heard the distant murmur of voices.

'Whoever you are so busy with,' he elaborated, totally ignoring the warning hand she raised to her lips.

Scarlet, who didn't want the world to know her business, closed the door. *'Whoever?'*

He shot her an impatient look and strode purposefully towards the bedroom door. Before Scarlet had any clue of his intention or could cry out in protest he yanked it open with such force it thudded loudly against the wall.

'You can't go in there!'

Ignoring her outraged yell, he stepped inside her bedroom. Breathless with anger, she brushed past him. 'What the—?' she began, planting her hands on her hips and glaring at him.

Roman O'Hagan is in my bedroom…talk about a reality-fantasy clash!

When Roman discovered no lover on the bed, but a neat pile of freshly laundered clothes on the bottom of a narrow single bed waiting to be put away, his sneering expression relaxed into bafflement.

'Where is he?'

The fantasy version had not involved him growling at her contemptuously. She pulled back in alarm as her thoughts shifted in the dangerous direction of what he *had* done. It wasn't soon enough to prevent a wave of warm, sexual lethargy working its way through her body.

'Where's who...?' She gave her head a little shake to focus her thoughts.

'The innocent act is quite unnecessary,' he assured her in a cold, clipped voice. 'It's nothing to me who you choose to sleep with.' Even as he said it it struck Roman rather forcibly that his behaviour suggested the exact opposite.

A disinterested observer who didn't know any better might actually have concluded he was the wronged lover. Making a conscious effort, he forced his hands to unclench.

Belatedly Scarlet caught his meaning; her eyes widened. 'You thought...' The low laugh began softly and increased to a full-blooded husky chuckle as the humour of the situation struck her.

She didn't know which was funnier: Roman O'Hagan, the man who had probably slept with more women than she had had hot dinners, having the nerve to get all sniffy because she was entertaining a man, or the idea that she was indulging in an evening of lust!

In these pyjamas too. She looked down at her casual but not sexy attire and released another low gurgle of mirth.

Roman inhaled, his nostrils flaring. 'You think this is funny?'

Scarlet stared at him incredulously. 'Not funny—*hilarious*—!' she corrected, cracking up again.

Bringing up Sam and holding down a full-time job did not exactly leave her with much time or energy for romantic adventures. Dating when you were a single mum was not a simple business and Scarlet had decided it simply wasn't worth the hassle.

As her laughter faded away she weighed the odds; he didn't *seem* drunk, but in view of a dearth of any other possible explanation for his presence, or his bizarre behaviour, she voiced her suspicions out loud.

'Have you been drinking?'

'I have not been drinking.' The denial was issued between clenched teeth.

'Do you mind? Entry to my bedroom is on an invitation-only basis.' She tossed her head and centred her scornful gaze on his devastatingly handsome dark face. 'And you're not invited.'

'I'm devastated.' The derisive look he gave her brought an angry glitter to Scarlet's eyes.

'You would be if you knew what you were missing!' she heard herself jeer.

'If that was an invitation, I'll pass,' he replied, continuing his suspicious visual examination of the room.

'It wasn't.' If he was going to insult her, the least he could do was look at her while he did it.

'You're alone?'

'And this would be your business because?'

He drew an exasperated breath. 'Are you totally incapable of answering a simple question?'

Scarlet shook her head in disbelief. 'I'm not answering any of your questions. Why on earth should I?'

He contemplated her belligerent face for a moment before saying in a placatory manner, 'We can take this into the other room if you prefer.'

Scarlet vented a brittle laugh as she followed him into the living room. '*Wow*, you're all consideration,' she drawled with mock admiration. 'You really have got the most incredible cheek. You barge in here uninvited. You let me think something has happened to Sam and then turn it around and interrogate me!' She gave a weary sigh. 'Will you just go?'

'It's seven-thirty.' His glance rested pointedly on her pyjamas. 'Why are you dressed for bed?'

'Oh, I always wear these when I plan an evening of seduction.'

Her sarcasm brought a dark line of colour to the slashing angle of his incredible cheekbones.

'Then you're alone?'

'I was,' she retorted drily.

He looked around the room, registering the blurred frozen image on the TV screen, the box of chocolates and the untouched glass of wine. His glance reached the box of toys tucked into a corner and he frowned.

'Is…?' He swallowed. 'Where is Sam?'

'Sam is sleeping over at a friend's, the *Bradleys*, which is probably just as well in the circumstances.'

'The circumstances being?'

'Three-year-olds don't react well to being woken up.'

'Ah.' His facial muscles clenched, exaggerating the sharp contours and angles of his face. He really did have bone structure to die for, she thought, despising the weakness that made her incapable of not staring. 'I didn't think.'

'About anything other than what you want? I'd already worked that one out. No doubt it's acting on impulse that makes you such a financial success?'

'I know you're not Sam's mother.'

She waited, her expression attentive but confused, until it occurred to her he was expecting some sort of response. 'Not his birth mother, no,' she agreed. The adoption had made her his legal guardian.

She was cool, he had to give her that. 'You didn't ask me how I knew you weren't his mother?'

She shrugged her shoulders and still betrayed none of the

guilt he had expected her to when confronted. 'I suppose I assumed someone mentioned it in passing. David, maybe?'

'David?'

'The vice-chancellor.'

'You call the vice-chancellor *David*?' His voice was heavy with suspicion.

'He went to school with my uncle, I've known him since I was a little girl so, yes, I do call him David.'

'And he knows Sam isn't your son?'

Scarlet shook her head in total bewilderment. 'It's not like it's a secret. Everyone knows, I suppose.'

He looked at her, his dark brows drawn into a straight line.

'Why? What did you think?'

His eyes were hidden beneath the lustrous sweep of his lashes as he looked across at her, but his attitude suggested he was wary. 'Then who is Sam's birth mother?'

'My sister Abby was Sam's mother.'

CHAPTER EIGHT

COMPREHENSION struck Roman with the force of a tidal wave. Of the scenarios he had imagined—and he had imagined plenty—this one had never occurred to him.

The people he employed on those occasions when he required a background check were both efficient and discreet. He could have had the information she had just provided in literally a matter of hours, maybe less. Instead he had taken a far more tortuous route, and had his DNA compared with the hair sample he had taken from the child.

At the time he had told himself that the fewer people who knew what he was doing, the less chance there was of the story leaking out. He'd wanted to know for certain he didn't have a son without having to involve a whole string of people. Now he was forced to consider the possibility that the *truth* had only been part of what he had wanted—he had wanted someone to blame.

Not just someone.

The stranger who was bringing up his child without his knowledge had to be guilty of *something*—! He had wanted to confront Scarlet, to make this personal—*it was personal*!

His stillness was scary, she thought. It was actually a relief when his shoulders lifted and a soundless sigh shuddered through his powerful frame.

'*Was…?*'

Scarlet looked away and with a gesture that was intensely weary rubbed the bridge of her nose; the glasses were gone but the habit remained. She blinked hard to clear her blurry vision as tears filled her eyes.

Damn—! She really didn't want to cry in front of him.

It wasn't as if she couldn't talk about Abby without getting upset; she made a point of talking about her with Sam, who had a photo of his mother in his room.

'Here, have this,' he said brusquely.

She released a wry laugh as she automatically took the glass he handed her. 'I was wondering if you ever say please?' she explained in reply to his questioning look.

A puzzled frown developed on her smooth brow as their glances meshed. 'Why are you here, Roman?'

'Your sister is dead?'

Scarlet nodded, and took a swallow of the wine.

'I'm sorry.'

'There's no need to be; you didn't know her.'

She caught a flicker of something in his expression that she couldn't put a name to, but it wasn't there when he walked back from the Welsh dresser with a clean mug in his hand. He proceeded to slosh some wine into it.

'It's cheap supermarket plonk.'

He looked at her, his piercing regard intense. He drew a deep breath and his hands coiled at his sides. 'You'd better sit down,' he said abruptly.

'People say that when they're about to tell you something you won't like hearing.'

He didn't deny it.

Scarlet moved a cushion and sat down on the sofa. Her stomach was churning with apprehension.

'You'd better sit down yourself,' she said with an irritable frown. 'You look terrible,' she added, observing the grey tinge to his olive-toned skin and the definite tautness in the lines around his mouth and eyes.

Her frown deepened.

He still looked pretty damned marvellous.

She watched as he did what she suggested, folding his

long, lean frame into a bucket chair beside the TV. It was laughably inadequate for his length and he ought to have looked silly but he performed the action with his usual inimitable grace. Scarlet loved to watch him move; clearly she was losing her mind.

'It upsets you to talk about your sister?'

Scarlet didn't hear him at first, because she was covetously watching him, imagining the shift of tight, hard muscles in his shoulders as he moved. He had unzipped his jacket and underneath he wore a simple white designer tee shirt. It was fitted enough to suggest the strongly defined musculature of his upper body, a strong body.

Her eyes were drawn to the faint shadow of body hair visible through the fine fabric and she had absolutely no control over the flutter low in her belly. An image of dark, smooth skin came into her head and she swallowed convulsively. It was like walking into a solid wall; the wave of paralysing longing that hit her made her head spin.

The situation called for her to face some facts she'd been ignoring. Since their first meeting she hadn't been able to get Roman out of her thoughts. At first she had tried to resist, but then she had told herself that indulging in the fantasies could do no harm. That had been a mistake, one which she was suffering for now.

She was obsessed!

Given full rein her fantasies had multiplied and got out of control. Now she couldn't look at him without her mind being filled by all kinds of erotic images her feverish imagination had conjured.

Well, it was about time she got her subconscious under control. She took a deep breath. They were talking about Abby, which made her preoccupation with sex all the more shameful.

'*Upset?* Not really, it just hits you sometimes...I miss

her,' she admitted simply. Abby wouldn't have thought her sexual fantasies shameful. If her sister had been here she would no doubt have advised her to go for it, she thought with a smile.

'Was there an illness…or an accident—?' There was nothing in his tone or attitude that she could put her finger on, but the question did not come over as a casual enquiry. 'You don't want to talk about it?' he asked.

'Not especially, but it would seem you do.' She picked up the cushion and hugged it tightly to her body, rocking a little as she pulled her knees up to her chest. 'Why is that? Did you know Abby?' Her eyes widened as she shot him a questioning look.

'I can't recall meeting an Abby Smith.'

'Oh, but Abby didn't use Smith. She said I looked like a Smith but she didn't—she was right,' she reflected, running a hand over the brown hair that Abby had always advised her to bleach. *Blondes darling, definitely have more fun!*

'She was an actress?'

Scarlet shook her head. 'She intended to be one day, but she was a model—Abby Deverell. She was quite successful. Well, actually, she was *very* successful.'

'Your sister was Abby Deverell?'

Scarlet could see him trying to find some similarity in her own features. It would be a fruitless search; Abby had been beautiful.

'People always do that, but we're not alike.'

God, the woman had had his child and he couldn't even recall her face clearly. What sort of man did that make him?

'So you did meet her?' Scarlet wondered why she hadn't considered the possibility earlier. It would certainly explain his brooding expression, she thought, slanting a surreptitious glance at his strong profile.

'Yes, I did meet her,' he returned abruptly.

Now he had a name and face...or he *should* have a face. The woman had fronted a very high-profile publicity campaign just a few years ago. You hadn't been able to walk down the street, open a magazine or switch on a television without seeing her face.

So why, when he tried now to visualise those photogenic features, was he only able to see the face of her younger sister?

Scarlet didn't register the abruptness of his reply. 'She was very lovely, wasn't she?'

He responded to her wistful appeal with an affirmative nod, not because he remembered, to his shame he didn't, but because it was obviously what she wanted to hear. 'Yes, she was.'

He had spent one night at her flat. He knew the date; it should have been his first wedding anniversary. He had woken up fully dressed on her sofa with a raging headache; she had said she had let him sleep it off.

'Did you know her well?'

His silence lasted a long time—a noticeably long time.

Scarlet drew a sharp breath as she suddenly went icy cold all over, convinced that he was about to admit they had been lovers.

'No, I didn't know her well.'

The sigh of relief that whistled through her clenched teeth was silent. If he had been Abby's lover, why would it have made a difference...? What was there for it to make a difference to? It wasn't as if there was, or ever would be, anything between her and Roman.

'So Sam knows you're not his real mother?'

'Of course. You shouldn't lie to children.'

'A very sound principle,' he approved smoothly. 'And when Sam's older and he asks about his parents you'll be able to tell him...?'

Unwittingly, she thought, he had touched upon a subject that had concerned her for some time. Sam would ask about his father, it was inevitable, but what was she supposed to tell him? The truth? Or was she to invent a hero that a boy could be proud of? It was a minefield.

'Sam's very young to understand yet.'

'It's surprising how much children understand.'

'I'll be able to tell him that his mummy loved him very much.'

'Has she been gone long?'

'Abby learnt she had leukaemia when she was first pregnant with Sam,' Scarlet recalled quietly. 'The doctors wanted her to have a termination and start treatment straight away. They warned her that not to do so would seriously reduce her chances of survival.'

Their eyes locked. The shock in his was visible, as was the compassion; the latter made her throat ache, and she swallowed.

'And they were right?'

'Yes,' she admitted softly.

'She ignored them?' he probed gently.

Scarlet nodded.

He released his breath in a long fractured hiss. 'What a decision to be forced to make.' And make alone.

'I don't think it actually was that hard for Abby. I don't think a termination was ever an option for her.'

'How long after?'

'Sam was three months old when she died; most of that three months she spent in hospital,' she imparted quietly.

Roman caught his breath. 'My God.' His brow furrowed. 'She *knew* that having her baby would kill her?'

Anger flared in Scarlet's dark-fringed hazel eyes. 'No, *leukaemia* killed her.'

She was painfully aware that it was possible for a careless

word to plant an idea in a child's head, and she determined that Sam wouldn't grow up burdened with the guilt of his mother's death.

'And I'd be grateful if you didn't say that again—*ever*.'

He inclined his head towards her. 'Of course, I'm sorry.'

Rather taken aback by his apparent sincerity, she accepted it with a grudging but wary nod.

'And you have brought her baby up?' She gave a tiny nod of assent, and his hand came up to his mouth before moving roughly along the angle of his hard, angular jaw.

The bare facts were he had got a woman pregnant and for whatever reason she had not felt able to tell him. That woman had died and if her premature death could not be directly attributed to the birth of his son it had definitely been a contributing factor.

It didn't matter what sort of spin you put on those facts, he did not emerge from the telling of this story looking good. If there was any victim here he wasn't it...not that there was any shortage of victims in this story.

'That must have been hard.' He winced inwardly at the triteness of his words.

'I was terrified of the responsibility at first,' Scarlet admitted. She gave a small laugh. 'I still am sometimes...' Her eyes lifted. 'Does that sound terrible to you?'

As soon as she'd asked the question Scarlet hated the fact she sounded as though she was asking for his approval.

He didn't reply, just continued to look at her with an odd intensity.

'It doesn't sound terrible at all,' he said finally. 'So don't beat yourself up.'

She blinked to clear her blurry vision. It was perverse that after surviving his insults she should be brought to the brink of emotional tears by his kindness.

'Wasn't there someone else you could have shared the responsibility with?'

Scarlet sniffed and dabbed her finger to a spot of moisture in the corner of her eye. 'There was just Abby and me, and our gran who died last year. She was pretty frail.'

He searched her open features, and realised that not only was she *not* canvassing the sympathy vote, she didn't have the faintest idea how poignant her statement sounded.

Dealing with people who normally had an agenda—people who wanted something from him—Roman found himself uniquely ill equipped when it came to a dialogue with someone who said what they meant. Someone who furthermore would have thrown anything he offered back in his face.

'There were no other relatives who could help?'

'No. My uncle and aunty are not really *children* people.'

'But surely they were better situated than you to bring up a baby?'

'Financially maybe, but it's not about money, is it?' she said, taking his agreement on something so fundamental as granted. 'They didn't have a family of their own out of choice,' she went on to explain.

'And I can't imagine them welcoming *anything* which stopped them jumping in the car and driving down to the South of France when they felt like it.' Her nose wrinkled as she looked reflectively at him and her head tilted a little to one side. 'They're a bit like you, really. They do whatever they like without having to consider anyone else…though you're younger, obviously.'

'But equally selfish,' he suggested drily.

'They love one another, so you can't call them *totally* self-obsessed and narcissistic,' she pointed out tolerantly.

'Unlike me.'

Scarlet flushed under his ironic gaze. 'I didn't say that,' she protested.

'You didn't need to. You can't imagine me with children?'

Scarlet frowned at the inflection in his voice. 'You're Italian Irish, aren't you?' She gave an offhand shrug. 'With that background I expect you'll have a big family one day, when you're ready.'

In her head she could see children with Roman's dark eyes and warm colouring running around…children just like Sam.

'Or when I've grown up?'

'I wasn't going to say that. I'm a realist.'

Roman grinned. 'You have a smart mouth.' Lush, lovely and incredibly kissable—!

The fact his dark, devastatingly gorgeous eyes were glued to her lips, and that he was no longer grinning, made Scarlet very nervous.

'I wouldn't worry—a lot of men never grow up. You're obviously enjoying playing the field.' And, my, did he show dedication. She tried to make up for her lack of judgement in speaking her mind with a brittle, blindingly insincere smile.

'But I expect one day you'll get bored with it, and when you meet someone…' Someone beautiful and talented to give him those golden babies.

'You don't sound very convinced.'

'You're right, I've always had my doubts about reformed rakes,' she confided. Her glance skimmed the strong, arrogant lines in his hard-boned features. And if anyone could accurately be described as a rake, it was him.

'Rakes?'

Scarlet, who was warming to one of her favourite themes,

nodded, barely registering the stunned expression on his handsome face.

'I know a lot of women think that with the love of a good woman, the good woman being them,' she qualified drily, 'even the most committed playboy will metamorphose overnight into a faithful husband.' She shook her head and gave an incredulous laugh at the ability of her own sex to fool themselves.

'But you don't share this view?'

'Look at me! Do I look like a hopeless romantic?' she demanded.

He took her reckless offer and there was an extremely uncomfortable interval while he considered the question and her face. The defiant angle of Scarlet's chin increased in direct proportion to the rapid thud of her racing heart.

Finally he delivered his judgement.

'I don't have one hell of a lot of hands-on experience with hopeless romantics but, yes, I'd say you do.'

His dry comment drew Scarlet's eyes involuntarily to the hands he referred to. His long, tapering fingers curled lightly over the arms of the chair; they were square-tipped, suggesting sensitivity and strength. Something low in her belly tightened as she looked at them and imagined them moving over softer, paler flesh.

Colour significantly heightened, she dragged her eyes clear. 'Well, I'm not, and,' she informed him with feeling, '*I'm glad*. I don't see how falling in love can fundamentally change a person's character. Call me a cynic, but, the way I see it, once a faithless love rat always a—' She broke off, her eyes widening. 'Not that I'm calling you a faithless...'

His eyebrows lifted. '*No?* If you say so.' His mobile lips formed a cynical smile as he shrugged.

It was pretty damned hard to refute her observations when

you had fathered a child on a one-night stand and didn't discover it until almost four years later.

In most people's book that qualified as love-rattish behaviour. The fact it had been an accident did not make him any the less an irresponsible bastard.

'Marriage means different things to different people. Some people are more...flexible...' she finished awkwardly.

'I take it "flexible" is a euphemism for sleeping around.'

Scarlet gave an uncomfortable shrug and wondered how on earth she had got onto this subject. 'I guess so.'

His nostrils flared as he looked at her. The expression of chilling hauteur on his dark patrician features sent a ripple down her spine.

'I don't think I'd be at all flexible at the idea of my wife sleeping with anyone else. I happen to consider fidelity an essential component of marriage.'

'Well, it just goes to show you never can judge by appearances,' she responded cheerily. 'Look at me—' she suggested.

When he did her lashes swept down in a protective gesture. 'I used to be the most important thing in my life. I had it all, the job, the flat, the car—'

'And you don't regret giving it up?'

'Not for one second. I earn peanuts by comparison now,' she admitted. 'Not that I ever earned the *serious* money Abby did, but on the plus side nobody treats *me* like I'm a piece of meat, and I don't have to live on lettuce leaves and cigarettes to stay stick-thin! Mostly people appreciate what I'm doing.' *Present company excluded.*

'So your sister left you well provided for?' At least she hadn't spent the last four years leading a hand-to-mouth existence in order to give his son a decent life.

His relief turned out to be premature.

'Abby earned, but she liked to spend too. But, yes, she

had put some money aside for Sam. It will pay for his education and there'll be a little bit left over for a nest egg for him.'

'So you have lived off what?'

'I live within my means, and I don't worry if I'm not wearing this year's designs. I mean, money isn't everything, is it?' A sudden bubble of laughter sprang to her lips. 'Actually, I suppose it is to you.'

'Sure, I sold my soul for a good return on my investments years ago,' he drawled.

'I wasn't being offensive…well, not intentionally, anyhow,' she added with a crooked smile. His rigid expression didn't thaw. 'It was a joke.'

His dark eyes swept across her face. 'Was it?'

'Yes!' she responded, exasperated that he seemed intent on over-dramatising a simple comment. 'You're rich, I'm not, so what I've never had I'm not going to miss, am I?' she pointed out simply.

'Do you plan to go back to your old job?'

'Who knows what the future holds? But it would be good in the immediate future if you revealed a reason for you being here.'

'I'm getting there.'

The ironic twist of his lips troubled her. If she was going to be honest, Roman worried her full stop.

'Where does Sam's father come into all this?' he said casually.

'There isn't one.'

He raised an ironic brow.

'Well, there is, but he isn't in the picture. And not just that one,' she added as he picked up a framed photograph taken of Sam on his first birthday.

This was the point when people who possessed the basics of social skills dropped the subject.

'Have you ever tried to contact him?'

Scarlet shook her head. 'I couldn't if I wanted to.'

'Why's that?'

'I don't know who he is.'

'Surely your sister told you. I'm assuming she knew the seriousness of her condition.'

'Oh, yes, she knew,' Scarlet confirmed bleakly. 'I did ask Abby, I was concerned—' She broke off with a self-conscious grimace. 'She said getting pregnant was her responsibility.'

'Even if it was a one-night stand, that doesn't make it any less the man's responsibility.'

Scarlet shot him a look bristling with suspicion. 'I didn't say it was a one-night stand.'

'Didn't you?' He sounded genuinely surprised. 'Are you sure?'

'Totally.'

'I must have assumed.'

CHAPTER NINE

SCARLET studied Roman with suspicious eyes, bristling at the implied criticism. 'Abby had lots of boyfriends, but she didn't sleep around,' she told him fiercely.

What she didn't tell him, what she had never told anyone, was how Abby, heavily drugged in the final painful stages of her illness, had confessed when pressed for the identity of the father that it hadn't been an accident, that in fact she had planned to get pregnant. That she had wanted a baby and had chosen a father, she just hadn't included him in the plan.

'What if he finds out?' Scarlet asked.

'The only way he'll find out is if someone told him and you don't know who he is.'

'But when he hears you've had a baby, won't it be bound to cross his mind?'

'I doubt if he'll hear, but I thought of that. I told him nothing happened.'

'He was there, Abby.'

'He'd already had several drinks by the time we got back to my place,' Abby recalled, displaying none of her younger sister's awkwardness when it came to discussing the intimate details. 'He actually got quite maudlin and sentimental; I don't think he even noticed I'd added Scotch to his coffee,' she ended on a self-congratulatory note.

Scarlet couldn't believe what she was hearing. 'You got him drunk!'

'But not incapable. Please don't look at me like that, Scarlet, it's not like I raped the man. He enjoyed himself, and I got the impression he had something he wanted to forget. That was why he'd been drinking in the first place…something to do with it being the anniversary of something, I think.'

'But he wasn't a stranger.'

'I didn't want just *anybody* to be my baby's father,' Abby reproached indignantly. 'I did my research beforehand.'

'How long had you been planning to do this, Abby?'

'Let's just say this wasn't an impulse. I finally accepted I was never going to meet Mr Right and settle down. My biological clock was ticking away. I thought about artificial insemination but you don't really get to choose the father that way, and I got pregnant straight off, the first time, which is just as well, because I doubt if…so it must have been meant to be, don't you think, Scarlet?' she asked wistfully.

Scarlet felt unable under the circumstances to tell her sister what she actually thought and so moderated her views. 'You don't think it might be a good idea to tell the father?'

'God, no, a baby would scare the pants off him and I had a hard enough time getting them off the first time. Sorry, Scarlet, I don't mean to embarrass you with the gruesome details.'

'But a baby needs a father.'

'You're thinking about inherited weaknesses…'

'Not specifically,' Scarlet said weakly.

'No worries there, the guy is about as genetically perfect as is possible. When I drew up my list—'

'You had a *list*?'

'Well, it seemed logical, and he was streets ahead of the rest,' Abby revealed, apparently oblivious that she was saying anything out of the ordinary. 'His family on both sides all seem to be disgustingly healthy and live until a ripe old age.'

'You seem to have thought of everything,' Scarlet responded weakly.

'You don't approve, do you, Scarlet? I knew you wouldn't but I was desperate. You have no idea how badly I wanted this baby.'

Scarlet tried to hide how desperately shocked she was when her weak and frail sister went on to describe how she had ruthlessly engineered the seduction to coincide with her fertile period and tampered with the condom! How could you condemn someone who was clinging to life? The guilt of being healthy and strong when someone she loved was dying by inches silenced any protest she might have made.

Abby's spontaneous, warm nature was part of what made her the lovable person she was. But being spontaneous and warm was one thing—what Abby had done was something else! As far as Scarlet was concerned, having a baby was the ultimate expression of love. There had seemed precious little love in the event that Abby described.

'What would you do if the father suddenly appeared?'

The sound of his voice brought Scarlet back to the present.

She blinked her eyes, focusing on Roman's lean, watchful features. Logically danger ought to repel any right-thinking person, but, while there was something distinctly wolf-like in his lean, hungry aspect, it was that same danger that exerted a strange, almost hypnotic attraction.

'I asked what you would do if Sam's father reappeared.'

'Sam's father?'

As always when she thought about the mystery man her sister had callously tricked she was engulfed by a wave of crushing guilt.

There had been a time when she had actually considered trying to discover who he was, but, short of putting an ad in the personal columns, when it came down to it she didn't have the faintest idea how to go about identifying him. And even if she did, would he thank her? According to Abby he was a man who, given the choice, would not have wanted to know—in fact a man who would have denied paternity.

In the circumstances it was academic. No, her energies were better concentrated on taking care of his son. The son he didn't know he had.

'That's not going to happen,' she told him quietly. There was nothing in his face to explain his motivation in pursuit of the subject.

'But the idea alarms you?'

Her eyes skimmed his face; she was unwilling to allow herself to become entrapped by his dark, mesmeric eyes. 'I didn't say that,' she countered quickly.

'You didn't need to—you have a very expressive face.'

Scarlet was immediately conscious of every facial muscle she possessed as she tried to produce a neutral expression. 'Trust me…I don't want to be rude, but none of this is actually any of your business.'

'It's Sam's father's business,' he replied after a taut silence.

'Sam's father is not going to materialise,' she promised him.

'But if he did…' Roman persisted. 'What would you do if he wanted to be part of Sam's life?'

It seemed much more likely that he would resent the child that he had been tricked into fathering, and who could blame him? Not Scarlet. Non-consensual fatherhood pretty much fitted what had been done to him.

'That's really not at all likely.' His unblinking, glittering scrutiny was making her increasingly nervous.

'Hypothetically,' he inserted smoothly.

'*Hypothetically* I'd work something out for Sam's sake, but this isn't something that's going to happen.'

PLAY THE
Lucky Key Game

Do You Have the LUCKY KEY?

and you can get

FREE BOOKS
and a FREE GIFT!

Scratch the gold areas with a coin. Then check below to see the books and gift you can get!

YES! I have scratched off the gold areas. Please send me the 4 FREE BOOKS and GIFT for which I qualify. I understand I am under no obligation to purchase any books, as explained on the back of this card. I am over 18 years of age.

P4FI

Mrs/Miss/Ms/Mr _____ Initials _____

BLOCK CAPITALS PLEASE

Surname _____

Address _____

_____

Postcode _____

🔑🔑🔑🔑 4 free books plus a free gift   🔑🔑🔑🔑 1 free book

🔑🔑🔑🔑 4 free books   🔑🔑🔑🔑 Try Again!

Visit us online at
www.millsandboon.co.uk

◄ DETACH AND POST CARD TODAY! ►

The Reader Service™ — Here's how it works:

Accepting the free books places you under no obligation to buy anything. You may keep the books and gift and return the despatch note marked 'cancel'. If we do not hear from you, about a month later we'll send you 6 brand new books and invoice you just £2.69* each. That's the complete price - there is no extra charge for postage and packing. You may cancel at any time, otherwise every month we'll send you 6 more books, which you may either purchase or return to us - the choice is yours.

*Terms and prices subject to change without notice.

THE READER SERVICE™
FREE BOOK OFFER
FREEPOST CN81
CROYDON
CR9 3WZ

NO STAMP
NECESSARY
IF POSTED IN
THE U.K. OR N.I.

'You sound very sure.'

'I am.'

'How can you be?'

'Abby didn't tell him,' she revealed abruptly.

'She knew who he was, then?'

Scarlet let out a furious gasp and bounced to her feet. The shocking sound of her hand connecting with his face resounded around the room.

She looked from her extended hand to the mark on his lean cheek. The thin white scar stood out lividly against the reddened skin. Her chest heaved with emotion as her eyes met his.

'You pack quite a punch.'

She had started shaking in reaction. 'I'm sorry.' She was deeply ashamed of the loss of control that had made her resort to violence. 'But you deserved it,' she added with a glare that dared him to disagree with her.

Roman levered himself from the chair in a fluid elegant motion. He looked down at her from his superior vantage point.

'Maybe I do.'

Scarlet looked up at him warily through the protective dark mesh of her lashes. This was not the reaction she had expected.

'What do you mean?'

'You recall when my mother collapsed at the opening ceremony?'

Scarlet nodded. 'Of course I do.' She had not the faintest idea where this was going and, call her a coward, but she didn't actually want to know.

'It was because she saw someone she recognised.'

She still didn't have an inkling. Her smooth brow pleated in a perplexed, wary frown. 'Who did she recognise?'

'She saw Sam.'

An image of Sam, the posy of wilting flowers clutched in his hot, sticky hands, flashed into her head. 'I don't understand.'

He scanned her face for a moment, his own expression broodingly sombre. 'I know you don't. Sam looks exactly the way I did when I was his age. That's what spooked my mother.'

Scarlet was confused but not suspicious, which later on struck her as ironic in the extreme. 'Because Sam looks like you?' Perhaps it was the colouring. Sam did have that Mediterranean glow and the long lashes and, now that she thought about it, at certain angles...

'Because Sam is my son.'

Scarlet was dramatically unprepared for his revelation, which, when at a later date she went over the conversation that had led to it, made her blind, deaf and very stupid!

She was not conscious then or later of his tensing and moving closer in readiness to catch her as the colour seeped rapidly from her skin, leaving it marble-pale.

'For God's sake, sit down.'

Quivering with denial, she kept to her feet. 'You and Abby?' She shook her head, feeling sick. 'You slept with Abby?' she wailed.

Now why did that make her feel as though she were the tragic victim of some betrayal? The victim here was Roman. What he must have felt like discovering he had a son this way she couldn't even imagine! Her well-developed sense of empathy sprang into life, as did her guilt.

'*Apparently.*'

Considering his admission, he was surprised when she didn't deliver the obvious comeback. To father a child accidentally was one thing, to forget about it took the crime to another level.

'She said not, but facts say otherwise,' he related grimly.

'That's ridiculous, you can't be!' she cried shrilly. 'She said he…*you*—' she corrected herself.

'She said what about me?'

Scarlet gave her head a tiny shake; she was having second thoughts about her candour. This was one occasion when the truth was not going to help.

'I don't recall exactly.'

'I'll settle for inexact.'

Scarlet gave an exasperated sigh; he wasn't going to leave well alone. She studied his profile. The light fell from behind, highlighting all the hard angles and intriguing hollows of his face.

'She said the father would have run a million miles if he'd known about the baby.'

Roman flinched.

'You're not running.'

'That's because she was wrong,' he breathed grimly. '*Very* wrong.'

Tears formed in Scarlet's eyes. 'Why are you saying this?' she choked, turning her hands palm upwards towards him in an unconscious gesture of appeal. 'What's the point?'

'*Point?*' he repeated, looking at her as though she were mad. 'I have a son.'

'You don't want Sam. You *can't*. Abby isn't here to punish so leave us alone.' Fighting the rising level of panic that made it hard for her to think, she covered her face with her forearm and swallowed a sob.

'Why would I want to punish the mother of my child? It was my fault.'

Scarlet, who could hear the self-recrimination in his voice, felt so guilty she could hardly look at him. Whatever else Roman was, he was clearly *not* the moral-free zone that Abby had taken him for.

'I'm hardly unable to support a son. Presumably she

thought I'd contest paternity and couldn't stomach the idea of the mud-slinging.' He raked a hand through his dark, sleek hair and fixed Scarlet with an interrogative stare.

She was too stunned by his reading of her late sister's motives that all she could do was stare at him. He appeared to take her silence as confirmation of his explanation.

Why couldn't he be the shallow, selfish playboy Abby had taken him for instead of the owner of a very well-developed set of moral principles? She didn't want to empathise with him, not when he might try and snatch Sam away from her.

She was her nephew's legal guardian but where would she stand legally if he chose to contest her guardianship?

Scarlet was terrified by the thought of a custody battle. Better to let him carry on thinking the pregnancy had been accidental than allow that to happen. Why tell him the truth when there was nothing to be gained except blackening her sister's name?

'Your sister may have been misguided in going it alone.' This admission seemed to be as close as he was going to get to criticising Abby. 'But you've got to admire her. Most women finding themselves in that situation would have wanted to make me pay.'

'Abby didn't want your money.' Her head lifted and there was a flicker of hope in her eyes. 'Couldn't you just pretend you didn't know?' she suggested with a sniff as she wiped the moisture from her face. 'I'm sure it would be a lot more comfortable for you and I wouldn't say anything to anyone.' She dabbed a stray tear from her cheek with the back of her hand.

'You expect me to pretend I don't have a son?' he grated. *'Dio!'* he ejaculated rawly. 'What sort of man do you think I am?' he demanded, every inch of his powerful frame vibrating at the affront.

Scarlet shook her head in a bemused fashion, unable even at this critical moment not to appreciate just how magnificent in a lean, mean way he looked when he was mad. When he lost his temper he was very much the Mediterranean male, all passion and fire.

'This is still just speculation. You can't prove it. Just because you slept with Abby doesn't mean you're Sam's father.' She clung stubbornly to the hope that this might still turn out to be a terrible misunderstanding.

'But DNA sampling does. I wouldn't have come to you unless I was sure. I took a hair sample, Scarlet, the day at the nursery, and had it analysed.'

She sank back into her chair, the fight draining out of her. 'Oh, my God!' she whispered, knowing what was coming.

CHAPTER TEN

'THERE is no doubt about it. Sam is my son, there's no question.'

Scarlet shook her head and, hand pressed to her mouth, ran towards the bathroom. 'Excuse me!' she gulped, polite to the end, and then she bolted.

She was in too much of a hurry to close the door behind her and Roman heard the sound of her painful retching. It was several minutes later when she returned, paler and graver, but her composure was obviously paper-thin.

'If you think you can take him off me… I know you've got money.'

Roman could almost see the sinister plan he hadn't made to snatch the child away from her forming in her mind.

'Don't be melodramatic.'

'I'll run away and you'll never find us,' she threatened wildly. *Now that makes me sound like stable, responsible parent material.*

'I can see you've cast me in the role of evil villain to your wilting heroine.'

'I've never wilted in my life.'

'I'm glad to hear it. I can't abide a clingy female.' He reached out and took her shoulders. When there was no resistance he drew her gently towards him. 'I'm not going to take Sam off you. I just want to be part of his life.'

And he had a right to be part of his life, but what sort of upheaval would that cause for Sam, not to mention herself. Scarlet didn't feel capable of working out the implications of this; she no longer knew which way was up, let alone what was a lie or the truth!

Scarlet, totally focused on convincing him she wasn't going to let him take Sam, didn't even feel the pain as her neatly trimmed nails gouged into the soft flesh of her palms.

'Sam's life is with me,' she asserted loudly.

Roman inhaled sharply and his hands fell from her shoulders. 'He is my son. This will be much easier, Scarlet, if we work together. If we're friends.'

'*Friends?* Even if none of this had happened we could never be friends,' she asserted hotly.

On this at least Scarlet could be totally confident. How could you be friends with someone whose way of life was a total anathema to you, someone with whom you didn't have anything in common and someone who, furthermore, made your hormones act in an indiscriminate and mortifying manner?

Irritation showed in his deep-set shadowed eyes as he heard her out.

'A little bit of give and take here—would it be too much to ask?' he wondered, dragging his hand wearily through his already disordered hair.

Scarlet experienced an irrational urge to smooth down those disordered locks. 'Me give Sam, and you take him! Sam is three—where were you when he had chicken pox? Were you there to hold his hand when they stitched up his head when he fell off his bike?'

'I didn't know I had a son.'

So far he'd only thought about the changes having a son was going to make to his life. For the first time he paused to consider the things he had already missed out on, things he would never see, like the child's first steps. He was unprepared for the feeling of profound loss.

'And now you do, so what? Are you going to change

your entire lifestyle?' *I don't think so.* 'It's obvious you haven't thought this through. What do you plan to do—fit Sam into your schedule between making your next million or wooing your next supermodel? You can't walk in here and demand to be part of Sam's life.'

'I'm not demanding anything.'

'That's not the way it looks from where I'm standing.'

'There are things I can give Sam.'

'Money—?' she suggested scornfully.

'Financial security, certainly,' he agreed levelly.

'Well, that was predictable. I wondered when the pound sign would start flashing.' She raised an eyebrow and produced a disdainful sniff. 'Well, you can put your chequebook away; we don't want your money,' she completed contemptuously.

There was a short simmering silence. Looking down his patrician nose at her, he drew himself up to his full height. 'Does it give you a nice sense of moral superiority to be able to throw my money back in my face?'

'You can't buy me,' she gritted defiantly.

'I'm not trying to, neither am I trying to score points. I'm trying to consider my son's best interests.'

'So am I!' she rebutted uneasily, aware that her responses were becoming increasingly childish.

'*Are you?* I'm a wealthy man—do you expect me to leave my son nothing?'

'Well…I…I hadn't thought…'

'Sam will be the main beneficiary as soon as my solicitor has drafted my new will,' he told her quietly.

She might want to reject his money, but Sam was his son. 'You want to make him a beneficiary. I suppose that's reasonable,' she admitted.

'I want to make him *the* beneficiary.'

'Oh!'

'There is no one else. Obviously I'll reimburse you for any—'

'I don't want reimbursing. Don't you understand? I don't want anything from you! I think you're—'

'Shall we leave your feelings towards me to one side for a moment?'

Scarlet deeply resented him taking upon himself the role of impartial reason. 'Feelings for you!' she parroted. 'I don't have any feelings for you one way or the other.'

'I'm perfectly aware I hardly come out of this looking good.' You couldn't defend the indefensible. 'But it takes two and your sister denied me the right of knowing my son.'

'You leave Abby alone!' Scarlet yelled. 'I'd say she knew what she was doing.'

'So you think she made the right decision?'

'Too right I do,' Scarlet responded with hardly a qualm about lying through her teeth. 'A spoilt, commitment-shy playboy is hardly most people's idea of father material.'

A muscle in his lean cheek clenched more obviously with each successive insult she flung at him. Scarlet knew she was being wildly unfair, but hitting back at him was a knee-jerk reaction she had no control over.

His face went blank, his eyes flat and cold as they scanned her face.

'This isn't a situation of my making, but I'm going to do the right thing whether you like it or not. You're going to have to work with me on this, Scarlet.'

He was obviously very comfortable with issuing ultimatums, but Scarlet was not at all comfortable about meekly acquiescing!

When he got bossy her automatic response was to do the opposite of what he said and, if at all possible, in a manner that would dent his air of ineffable superiority.

'And if I don't?' People must have been doing what he said all his life to make him so damned sure of himself.

His shoulders lifted expressively as his eyes moved briefly across her faintly flushed face. 'We both want what is best for Sam, so you will.'

Scarlet felt a shiver trace its icy path up her spine. The silky words held an unmistakable threat and, even though he never deliberately used his undoubted physical presence to intimidate, it was hard not to be daunted by his tenacity.

'If you wanted what was best for Sam you'd go out that door and forget we exist,' she charged in a furious hiss.

'It's not going to happen.' His tone was not without sympathy, but there was no room for negotiation in his manner. The expression on his lean face was totally implacable. 'I have a son, Sam has a father and a family who will all want to know him. Are you going to deprive him of that?'

She blinked, an expression of confusion spreading across her face. How often had she wished that she could offer Sam a large, loving family? 'Do your family know about Sam?'

'My mother doesn't need the results of a DNA test; she was totally confident from that first moment she saw him that Sam is my son. She's completely over the moon about having a grandchild. I would imagine the champagne is even now on ice.'

'And will she have told your father?' Despite herself, Scarlet found herself interested by his colourful background.

Roman shook his head.

She got the impression he didn't want to discuss his father. It was only a feeling, his cloaked expression was unrevealing, but it was enough to make her speculate.

'But he's not going to be happy about having a grandchild?'

'My father is an inflexible and obstinate man. You understand him better if you accept one thing: he is blind to shades of grey. For Dad things are either right or wrong. You can safely assume that having a child outside marriage will fall into the *wrong* category.'

'He would reject Sam?' The thought that anyone could wish to punish a child for what they, in their narrow-minded way, perceived as the sins of the parents brought a ferocious, protective scowl to her face.

'No, of course not.' Impatiently he brushed aside her anxiety.

His response seemed spontaneous enough, but Scarlet remained unconvinced. Sam's grandfather sounded pretty scary and not at all nice.

She shook her head slowly from side to side. 'You mean not on the surface, that he'll be acting one way and feeling another…?' She shook her head with even more vigour as she thought about it. 'There is no way I'm having Sam exposed to that sort of atmosphere.'

'Dad isn't intolerant.'

'Isn't that slightly contradictory? You're the one who called him "inflexible" and "obstinate".'

'He'd probably say the same thing about me.'

His candour took her aback. 'Well, he doesn't sound like an ideal role model for a little boy to me.'

Roman adopted a mock bewildered expression. 'How can you say that when you can see how well I've turned out?'

Scarlet frowned. She hated it when he made fun of himself that way; it made him almost likeable. She knew it was very important not to like him.

'You don't get on with your father?'

Would it do Sam any favours to be accepted into the bosom of this dysfunctional family? Or am I just grasping at straws? Looking for a reason, any reason, not to co-

*operate when deep down I know full well I have no right to
deny Sam a father and an extended family.*

'That hardly makes me unique, but, yes, we disagree on
most things. My father holds some firm views on everything
including modern morals—mine mostly.' He rotated his
head as if to relieve the tension in his shoulders.

'That's silly; surely he knows most of the stuff in the
papers is exaggerated to sell newspapers.' Dear God, if you
took every article about him seriously he could be in Paris
and New York at the same time!

'Scarlet Smith…are you defending me?' He studied her
for several seconds before adding, without the mockery that
had laced his previous comment, 'I'm touched.'

Their eyes collided and Scarlet blushed to the roots of
her hair. 'Everyone knows that you should take the celebrity
stories with a pinch of salt,' she retorted crossly.

Her face got even hotter and her scowl even fiercer as he
continued to look at her, one dark brow raised.

'My father believes there's no smoke without fire,' he
commented after a painfully long pause—painful for Scarlet
anyway.

'People do and I suppose his generation—'

'Sure, there is the generation gap, but it's more than that,'
Roman interrupted. 'Before he met my mother, Dad had
planned to enter a seminary.'

Scarlet's eyes widened. '*Seminary?* Isn't that where you
train to be a priest?'

'It is,' Roman confirmed.

'Gracious!' she exclaimed unthinkingly. 'No wonder he
doesn't approve of you!'

'You and he will get on famously,' Roman predicted
drily. 'There's also…' Betraying an uncharacteristic inde-
cisiveness, he stopped and raked a hand through his dark
hair. 'Well, you might as well hear the story from me as

you'll undoubtedly hear a version of it from my father when you meet him.'

Scarlet was so curious she let the assumption that she would one day meet O'Hagan senior pass without comment.

'I was engaged to a girl—Sally.'

Her eyes widened. '*You* were engaged?'

'Yes, about five years ago. Why so surprised, Scarlet? Most men of my age have had at least one serious long-term relationship.'

'But I thought you were…'

'A shallow, womanising pig?' he suggested. He observed the surge of guilty colour in her cheeks with a cynical smile. 'Relax, there's no need to totally retrench, the two are not necessarily mutually incompatible.'

'Did your father not approve of her?'

'Far from it, he adored her. He still does. I'd known Sally since we were children—her parents are tenant farmers on the estate. We were always in and out of each other's houses.'

'The girl next door?'

He nodded. 'There was nothing then, but we met up at college and were involved briefly, but it was nothing heavy. Then a few years later we met up at a party. A month later we were engaged. My family, especially my father, was over the moon,' he recalled.

'But you couldn't go through with it.'

Roman's dark, saturnine features clenched. His lip curled into a self-derisive smile as their eyes met.

'No, actually *she* couldn't go through with it. She ran off on the eve of the wedding with my best man.'

'*Gracious!* That's…that's…' She gave a helpless shrug. Very little he could have told her could have shocked her more. Any response seemed hopelessly inadequate. 'I'm sorry. That must have been awful for you.'

'I've had better days, but it happened a very long time ago.'

Despite his apparent indifference Scarlet couldn't help but wonder if behind that casual attitude he was hiding his true feelings. Did he still love this woman who had dumped him so ignominiously? Had he gained his playboy reputation as a result of trying to forget his lost love?

'I don't understand. If she dumped you how come your father blames you?'

'There was a note. She asked me not to tell her parents until she had a chance to talk to them. I'm assuming she never did. Nobody but Mother and I know she ran off with Jake.'

'But—'

'It didn't last…she left for France and came back three weeks later alone. As far as my father is concerned I had the perfect woman and I drove her away. Maybe,' he mused, 'he was right. There's a possibility that you'll meet her in Ireland—she's a teacher at the local primary school these days.'

'When you meet up…' she began, then the implication of his words hit home. 'I won't be going to Ireland.'

'I'm sure Sam will be a lot more comfortable if you do.'

'That's moral blackmail!' she accused angrily.

'It's also common sense,' he pointed out. 'Don't worry, my parents will love Sam,' he promised in a warmer voice. 'There's no sinister reason I haven't spoken to my dad yet, I simply wanted to sort out things with you before I spoke to him.'

'"Sort out?"' she repeated, her mouth forming a twisted smile as she angrily studied his lean face. *As if I can be filed away like a completed contract.* 'Are we *sorted* now?' she asked bitingly.

'I simply meant…' Their eyes made contact, his lashes

came down, but not before she had seen the seething frustration in those dark depths. 'You are one prickly female, do you know that?'

'I don't like the idea of being *sorted*.'

'It's a figure of speech.'

'Then maybe you should choose your words with more care.'

'Dear God, I'm already walking on eggshells around you,' he claimed. 'The next logical step would be for us to communicate through a third party. Think about it,' he suggested heavily. 'All I knew for sure when I came here was Sam was my child, and you weren't the mother. I needed some answers.'

'What did you think I'd done, kidnapped him…?' she suggested sarcastically.

'I hadn't ruled out anything. As I've already said, all I knew for sure was you weren't the mother.'

'How convenient I'm not beautiful and blonde,' she jeered. 'Or you might not have realised it was impossible for me to be Sam's mum.'

A dark line of anger appeared along the crest of his cheekbones as their eyes made contact. His were darkly furious as they narrowed to angry glittering slits.

'I'm beginning to think there's an element of jealousy in your hostility.'

'"Jealousy?"' she parroted shrilly. 'You think I'm jealous that you slept with my sister? You must be mad.' Her scornful laugh had a hollow sound to it.

'I was thinking more along the lines of you being jealous because there is someone else with a claim to Sam and you're possessive, you want to keep him all to yourself. But if the other works?' One dark brow quirked suggestively.

A scorching flush travelled over her entire body as she gasped into the static silence that followed his words.

'I wouldn't sleep with a man like you if my life depended on it!'

'Not very original,' he mused, his hooded eyes trained on her heaving bosom. 'But you get full marks for conviction,' he commended.

His tone of amused condescension made her want to throw something large and heavy at his smug face. She hadn't expected the news she didn't want to sleep with him to send him into a deep depression, but there was no need for him to treat it like a joke.

'And,' she continued contemptuously, 'if *I* was choosing a father for my baby, *you* wouldn't even make the list!' She stopped, an expression of horror stealing across her face as she drew back from the very brink of revealing her sister's shameful secret.

As much as Scarlet didn't like the man, she didn't dislike him enough to rub his nose in the humiliating fact that, far from getting accidentally pregnant, her sister had planned the entire thing. If he did go on to become part of Sam's life—and, while she wasn't ready to admit that out loud just yet, deep down she knew it was going to happen—what would she do then? How was she to know that revealing the truth would not colour any relationship father and son might come to have?

Would Roman feel differently about his son if he knew he had been tricked and used…? It wasn't inconceivable a man could resent a child born of such circumstances. No, she decided, nothing could be achieved from coming clean.

For several moments Roman remained silent. When he finally responded he no longer appeared in the mood to be diverted by her comments.

'Having Sam provides you with the perfect excuse for you not getting out there, doesn't it?'

She responded with a grimace of genuine confusion to his observation. '"Getting out there?"'

'Have you always been scared of relationships?'

'You think I use Sam as an excuse? That I'm commit-ment-phobic?' She released an incredulous laugh. 'What you know about relationships could be printed on a match-box. And if by "getting out there" you mean joining the singles scene and hanging out in bars waiting to be picked up, I'm really not that desperate.'

'I'm happy for you. I wish I could say the same myself, but this conversation is enough to make anyone desper-ate—' He broke off and heaved a deep sigh. 'Do you think we could concentrate on the main objective of this conver-sation?'

She watched as he linked his hands behind his head and dropped his head back, the action exposed the long, pow-erful length of his brown throat. Her tummy muscles quiv-ered.

'What is the main objective of this conversation?' she asked huskily.

Roman unlinked his hands and let them fall to his side. 'I'd like to get to know my son, and before you say anything hear me out.' Their glances locked and slowly, grudgingly, Scarlet nodded. 'I don't expect this thing to happen over-night. Obviously it will be better for Sam if I become part of his life slowly…gradually.'

'If you become part of Sam's life, you're going to become part of mine.'

'Exactly,' he agreed, not reacting to the horror etched on her face. 'Which is why I thought you might have some ideas on the subject.'

Scarlet stared at him incredulously. *'Are you kidding? After what you've just thrown at me I can't even think straight!'*

'Well, we'll just have to put our heads together, won't we?' he gritted.

'I wouldn't be seen dead with any part of my body within thirty feet of the corresponding part of yours!'

His features tautened. 'Listen, my tolerance levels on this are pretty high because I know you think I'm a bastard. That I can accept,' he said heavily. 'But we need… You've got to think of Sam,' he reproached sternly.

As if she had been thinking of anything else for three years! He didn't have the faintest idea.

'You've got to stop turning this into something personal.'

Scarlet planted her hands on her hips and threw her head back. She was literally trembling with reaction.

'Wanna bet?' she drawled.

'Right, you want personal…fine.' He covered the space between them and grabbed the back of her head with one hand; with the other he framed her face. She looked at him with eyes wide and shocked; she smelt of flowery soap, shampoo, and warm woman, and Roman's body reacted violently to the combination.

'Is this the sort of personal you had in mind?'

Even while he was saying it the voice in the back of his head was telling him he'd been looking for an excuse to do this ever since he'd met her. Once he started kissing her the voice wasn't telling him anything, because his brain took a back seat.

In the moment before her soft lips parted to allow his tongue to slide deep inside her warm mouth he heard, or rather felt, the broken whimper in her throat. The erotic little rasp sent a lick of heat through his blood and a corresponding jolt through his already rock-hard body.

She melted into him like warm butter. There was no hint of resistance in the body he had drawn against his, just heat and softness and the promise of more. Greedily he accepted the sweetness so unexpectedly offered him and it was only several hot, frenzied heartbeats later that he lifted his head.

The effort to do so was physically painful.

They didn't immediately step apart, just stood, bodies leaning into each other, breathing hard. Roman's fingers were still meshed into the shiny strands of slightly damp hair on her head and she had hold of his shirt in both hands.

When the drumming in his ears got quieter he could make out the words she kept repeating over and over. 'Oh, my God…oh, my God…!'

'Right, that was stupid,' he said, leaning his chin against the top of her head. 'But inevitable,' he added half to himself. 'Considering the level of attraction.'

His comment succeeded in jolting Scarlet free from the sensual lethargy that had engulfed her. With a cry she tore free of him and backed away, her angry eyes fixed on his taut features.

'The only thing that's inevitable between us is mutual antipathy.' She rubbed her hand across her reddened, swollen lips. The action was purely symbolic; she didn't believe for a moment it would succeed wiping away the memory of his searing kiss.

She had never been kissed that way before, not in a way that had made her crave more than air the pressure of someone's lips on her own. It made her dizzy and breathless all over again to think of his tongue stroking inside her mouth.

His eyes trailed across her face, lingering on the soft, swollen contours of her full lips. He shrugged. 'If you say so,' he said thickly.

'Don't use that patronising tone with me,' she flared, wrenching her hungry gaze from his face. This wasn't the time to indulge in a staring match. 'And don't treat me like a child.'

As she glared straight ahead her eye-line was on a level

with his powerful chest. A chest that moments ago her breasts had been crushed against, softness against iron hardness. Her body had been plastered so close to his that she had been able to feel the heavy thud of his heart mingled with her own. Her eyes lifted as she tried to drag her thoughts clear of the dangerous memories.

Far from saving her, the retreat brought her eyes into direct contact with Roman's dark, deep-set, very angry eyes. Her lashes came down but not before a wave of sheer sexual longing had nailed her to the spot.

'Then don't act like one,' he advised, his manner clipped and impatient. 'I don't force myself on women.'

Scarlet shook her head to clear the sensual fog that made it hard for her to think straight. 'Hell, no, you're irresistible,' she husked sarcastically. 'You don't have to.' *Well, not with me, he doesn't.*

The memory of her total surrender was terrifying. One kiss and she'd been his to do anything he wanted with. She had never relinquished control that way in her life and if the memory of it wasn't enough to terrify her, the fact that she had liked feeling that way, that part of her wanted to recapture the feeling, was!

His jaw tightened another notch in response to her sarcastic jibe. 'You can't pretend that you were some sort of unwilling participant.'

Can and will, Scarlet thought, responding to his claim with a provocative shrug of her slender shoulders.

'That you didn't want to kiss me as much as I wanted to kiss you,' he continued between gritted teeth. 'That neither of us wanted it to stop. You can't pretend those things and expect me to treat you seriously, can you?' By the time he had finished the incredulity in his voice had become scorn.

She looked away from his relentless hard stare and gulped. It had been pretty foolish of her to assume that a man who possessed his vast experience of women would not know how she had felt.

'Like you said, it was stupid.' It was clearly pointless to keep up the illusion that she hadn't kissed him back.

A speculative expression slid across his dark features. 'Possibly…'

She shot him a startled look. 'What do you mean, ''possibly''?' she demanded suspiciously. 'There is no way we can go around kissing without it…' Roman raised a quizzical brow as she stopped, flushing to the roots of her hair with mortification.

'Not without it leading to other things,' he finished for her smoothly. 'I realise that.'

Her chin lifted. 'It's not that I couldn't have stopped.' The question was *when*?

'You just didn't want to.' A faint, strangled sound was the only thing that could get past the emotional thickness in Scarlet's throat. 'Neither did I,' he added.

Her eyes widened at his earthy admission.

Their eyes locked. His were filled with a raw hunger that snatched the breath from her lungs. She felt dizzy, and her stomach dipped as though she'd just stepped into a bottomless black hole. The whooshing sound in her ears intensified the sensation of light-headedness.

'You didn't…?' She flushed with mortification to hear the amazed delight in her voice.

It doesn't take much to please you, does it, Scarlet? A man saying he didn't want to stop. As if that is such a life-changing occurrence? Of course he hadn't wanted to stop. Men never did; it was in their nature. They took what was on offer.

Well, I'm not on offer! Once more with a little more conviction, Scarlet.

While she was still thinking he took action and a step that

brought him closer, close enough for her to smell the warm male scent that rose from his body. The smile, the dangerous confident smile on his face kick-started her pulse. Now was the time to tell him she wasn't interested, spell it out once and for all.

She instinctively knew that with Roman saying no would be enough.

She opened her mouth to speak but nothing came out to break the silence. His movements were unhurried, deliberate even, but for Scarlet he seemed to move in slow motion. She wasn't aware that she had been holding her breath until he took her face between his big hands.

Her breath escaped in a series of uneven gasps as his brown fingers moved along the curve of her jaw.

'You have lovely hair,' he rasped, releasing the clip that confined her curls on top of her head. Quite deliberately he fanned it out around her face, running his fingers through the silky damp strands.

'No.' She shook her head. 'It's brown.'

Roman paused in the act of sliding his hands down her back. A baffled expression crossed his handsome face. 'This is something you need to apologise for?'

'And it's too fine. I can't do anything with it.'

She felt his laughter. 'Brown and fine suits your face.'

He tilted her head back to inspect the face he referred to. Scarlet was very conscious of his other hand, which was resting very firmly on the curve of her bottom.

'A nice face,' he decided just before he kissed her.

Scarlet gave a sigh as all the strength left her limbs. She had no choice or, for that matter, desire to do anything but let her body mould itself to his lithe, lean male frame.

'Please…Roman,' she moaned when his head lifted. She buried her own in his shoulder with a muffled sob.

He placed a finger under her chin and tilted her face up to him. 'Please what?'

'This is stupid. You know this is stupid. Things are complicated enough without putting...' the colour deepened in her cheeks '...*this*,' she added with an agonised grimace, 'into the equation.'

'*This* is not going to complicate things,' he contradicted, running a finger over the downy soft curve of her cheek. A distracted expression drifted over his hard, strong-boned features. 'God, but your skin is so soft,' he marvelled, his voice a deep, throaty purr. 'So incredibly soft.'

Scarlet dragged his hand from her face. It was so large compared to hers, his brown fingers long and tapering, she could feel the definite suggestion of calluses on his palm. These were not the hands of a man who was desk-bound.

As if reading her mind he offered an explanation. 'The gym bores me. I prefer to climb; it helps me concentrate.'

Once he'd said it she had no problem seeing him clinging to a rock face, using a combination of skill, strength and recklessness, pitting himself against a rock face and the elements, solo because he was not a natural team player.

'There's not much climbing to be had in London.'

'There are some very good climbing walls, though, and I don't live in the city all the time.'

Responding to a sudden crazy impulse, she raised his hand to her mouth and pressed an open-mouthed kiss into his open palm.

She felt his sharp inhalation and with a self-condemnatory groan dropped his fingers as though burnt, which in a way she was. The expression 'playing with fire' could have been created specially to cover this situation.

'Sorry!' she said in an agonised whisper. 'I shouldn't have. This is not sensible.'

A reckless-sounding laugh was wrenched from his throat. 'Who needs sensible?'

Scarlet lifted her head. 'Me.'

His dark, glittering eyes scanned her face. 'Fine, then look at it this way. Let's *use* what we're feeling.'

Scarlet managed to drag her eyes from his mouth. Her brain felt slow and stupid as she parroted, '"Use" it? Use what?'

'The fact there is a strong sexual attraction.'

'I don't understand.'

'What do you normally do when you feel this way?'

A difficult question to answer honestly when she had never felt this way before. She had never longed to plaster herself against a man she barely knew; she had not fantasised about feeling his weight on top of her or wanted to explore every inch of his body with her hands and lips. Honesty was clearly not an option here.

'I don't *do* anything. I'm too busy for relationships and I don't do one-night stands.' She could understand it if he found her last claim difficult to believe after the way she'd behaved.

'I doubt if one night would be sufficient.' Roman slanted her a heavy-eyed look of such sensuous promise that her knees trembled. 'You would date the guy…right?'

'"Date…?"' she echoed as though he were talking a foreign language. 'You're not suggesting me going to dinner or the movies with you is going to help anything?'

'When you are attracted to a man and the feeling is reciprocated that is what most people do…though *dinner* is not essential and personally I'm adaptable and could skip this preliminary stage of the mating ritual.'

'Too much detail!' she interrupted, holding up her hand to halt the flow of information and shaking her head vigorously from side to side.

'Think about it. Sam needs to get to know me, but not in a forced, fake way. If we were dating—'

'Which we're not.'

'If I was the new boyfriend we'd be bound to spend time together.'

He sounded so damned pleased with himself Scarlet was torn between laughter and hysterical tears. 'You're serious, aren't you? You want me to pretend we're going out together so you can get to know Sam.'

Me the girlfriend of Roman O'Hagan—sure, and the world really is going to believe that. Heavens, even a three-year-old would see through that one!

'Not pretend, no.'

The colour seeped out of her face and then flooded back. 'You can't be serious.'

'Sam must be used to seeing your boyfriends around the place?'

She shook her head, still stunned by his suggestion. 'No, he isn't.'

'Don't you have a social life, then?' he asked, clearly not taking her statement at face value.

'Of course I have a social life. I go to a yoga class and I belong to a quilting—'

His dark brows twitched. '*Quilting?* I frequently can't tell if you're on the level or you're trying to wind me up.'

'I don't see why me talking about quilting can possibly be considered trying to wind you up.'

'I'm not talking about *quilting*!' he exploded.

'Quilting is very relaxing,' she informed him with dignity. 'And you have something pretty and practical to show for your efforts at the end of the day. I've not got very far yet, but just because you've no aptitude for something doesn't mean you shouldn't stick with it.'

'I am sticking with it but I can't guarantee for how long.

Will you quit talking about quilting?' he revealed in a low, driven tone. 'I'm talking about sex, unless you've taken some vow of celibacy. Please tell me you've not,' he begged.

An expression of shock spread across his face when, instead of sharing the joke, she looked away. 'You don't date...not at all?'

'Of course I date.'

'I don't see what the problem is, then. Why not date me?'

When he said *'date me'* she was pretty sure it was a euphemism for *sleep with me*. 'You don't see the problem because you're a sandwich short of a picnic and unused to dealing with rejection.'

'Rejection I can deal with, but not from a woman who starts trembling with desire and undressing me with her eyes every time she's in the same room as me.'

The mortified heat rushed to her cheeks. 'My God, you are so colossally arrogant,' she breathed.

A wolfish grin split his dark lean features as he looked down into her outraged face. 'Maybe I am, but also I'm right. Aren't I, Scarlet?'

Scarlet wasn't going down that road.

'You want reasons? Let me see—where shall I start? How do you know I don't already have a boyfriend?'

'You said you don't have time for boyfriends.'

'Well, I don't.'

'That probably explains your short temper.' His fuse was certainly getting extremely short.

He could trace the source with great precision to the moment he had walked into her office and found her struggling into that too-tight top. When you lived in a society where you were constantly bombarded with images of provocatively undressed women it was kind of ironic that he had got so totally hung up over a one-blink-and-you'll-miss-it glimpse of bare flesh.

'Everything is about sex with you, isn't it?' she accused. 'You're obsessed,' she condemned crossly.

It took something as simple as a throw-away comment sometimes. His dark eyes trailed across her face, the soft contours of which he knew were already fixed in his memory. So was the sound of her laugh and her glare and the way...in fact he could access all her facial expressions any time he liked and also sometimes when he didn't like.

'You might not be wrong there,' he agreed.

'I don't know what you mean.'

'I think you do. I think you also know how good sex could be for us,' he rasped in a throaty voice that turned the heavy feeling low in her belly into an actual ache. 'But for some reason you're denying it.'

She closed her eyes and counted to a hundred slowly; all it did was panic her into impetuous speech.

'Actually I don't know a damned thing about sex,' she heard herself announce loudly. 'And before you offer I don't want any lessons from you.'

'Lessons...now that conjures up some very interesting—' He stopped dead, the teasing expression fading dramatically from his face. Eyes narrowed, he subjected her to a hard, searching scrutiny. 'Good God!' he ejaculated hoarsely. 'You're a virgin.'

CHAPTER ELEVEN

'WHETHER I am or not is totally irrelevant and none of your business,' Scarlet was driven by sheer embarrassment to retort.

'It won't be irrelevant to the guy who sleeps with you,' Rowan promised grimly.

Scarlet heard the shaken note in his voice. Well, she'd wanted to turn him off and it would seem she'd succeeded.

'Obviously that changes things,' he added soberly.

Scarlet glared at him indignantly. 'I don't see why. I may not be *vastly* experienced, but I think I'd manage to keep up with you. How hard can it be?'

Something moved at the back of his eyes in response to her challenge. 'There's only one way to find out.' He heard the words come out of his mouth but still he couldn't believe he'd been responsible for them. *A virgin? I'm mad out of my head, insane.*

He watched the rapid rise and fall of her breasts, her lips slightly parted and rosily moist and her eyes—eyes that were frequently a mirror image of her mood—sparkling with reckless challenge.

'What have you been doing—waiting for the right man?' he blasted, suddenly mad as hell with her.

Scarlet blinked, bewildered by his anger. 'Well, that rules you out!'

A nerve jumped along his hard jaw as he leant closer, his voice soft in her ear. 'I may not be the right man, Scarlet, but maybe I'm the wrong man? Sometimes the *wrong* man, like the forbidden fruit, can be more exciting.'

Mesmerised by the erotic rasp of his low voice and spectacular pitch-black smouldering eyes, she stared up at him so painfully excited and aroused she had to fight for each individual breath. Her body, every inch of her skin was burning, trickles of moisture formed in the hollow between her breasts and tiny trickles ran down the smooth skin of her back.

'I...I...' she stuttered, staring at him in undisguised longing. He was so beautiful she wanted to cry; he was so beautiful she wanted to beg him to touch her. Her mind was so consumed by desire that she had no other thought in her head but assuaging the hunger inside her.

He touched the side of her face, and looked into eyes wide and startled. Scarlet returned his stare before sucking in a deep breath and closing her eyes tight to shut out his probing stare.

She felt as if her feelings were written in neon a mile high across her face. She loved him. She who had always scoffed at the idea of love at first sight had fallen madly, deeply and irrevocably in love with Roman O'Hagan.

His fingers barely brushed her skin yet a moan was drawn from deep in her throat. She felt him take her hands within his and she lifted her head. He was standing over her. She trembled as he unfurled her tightly clenched fingers before placing both her hands palm down against his chest. She felt the ripple of taut muscles beneath her fingers and the last vestiges of restraint melted away in the heat of arousal.

Drawing a deep breath, she splayed her fingers and deepened the exploration of the hard male contours. She could feel the heat of his skin through the fine fabric of his shirt.

'You're totally incredible,' she breathed.

'I want your hands on me.'

Scarlet, her tongue caught between her teeth as she concentrated all her senses on the tactile sensation, slid her fingers through the inviting gap between the buttons.

'You're warm,' she whispered, trailing one finger slowly along the hard but incredibly smooth muscled ridges of his perfectly developed chest down to his flat belly.

With a mumbled hoarse imprecation Roman took hold of the expensive fabric of his shirt and pulled. There was a harsh ripping sound and buttons flew across the room.

'Your shirt!' she protested.

'I've got other shirts.' With a shrug he dismissed the damaged article that hung loosely open to his waist. 'However I've only one mind and if you don't touch me it could be permanently damaged,' he claimed, taking her wrist.

Scarlet only spent a moment wondering what he was going to do before he placed her hand palm-flat against the broad expanse of softly gleaming golden flesh his violent action had exposed. She felt the sharp contraction of taut muscles beneath her hand and her own stomach muscles spasmed as if in sympathy.

His warm, fragrant breath brushed her sensitive earlobe as he inclined his dark, glossy head. 'No, not *warm*,' he contradicted. '*Hot*. You,' he confided huskily, 'make me hot. From the moment I saw those delicious little breasts of yours I wanted to taste them. I wanted…'

Scarlet, who felt light-headed and strangely removed from what was happening, smiled; it was a smile of anticipation. Perhaps it was that distance, that sense of unreality that enabled her to respond with such devastating honesty? Or maybe something in her instinctively recognised that the situation warranted some plain speaking. Either way she knew this wasn't the time to be sensible or cautious.

Hell! Hadn't she had a lifetime of being both? Didn't she deserve just a little madness?

'No, don't say it,' she begged, directing her passion-glazed slumberous stare to his face. *'Do it!'* she commanded, reaching up to greedily sink her fingers in his hair. The dark waves were ebony and slippery like silk, but she clung hard, yanking his face down to her level.

'It hurts,' she told him, pressing her mouth hard against his. Her eyes were glittering with a feverish brilliance when her head lifted.

'What hurts?' he asked raggedly.

'Wanting to touch you hurts. I've never wanted anything or anyone as much as I want you,' she revealed starkly.

For a long sizzling moment their glances froze, the mutual message of hunger between them a palpable entity. His gasp, the one that moulded his belly into a tight, concave curve, was part of the same fluid movement that scooped her up into his arms.

Scarlet's arms looped about his neck, her legs locked tight around his middle, she kissed him with all the fervour of a mouse totally determined the cat *would* catch her as Roman bore his burden in the general direction of the bedroom.

They collided with several large items of furniture, knocked over a lamp, a framed picture and sundry items, but neither registered the destruction they left in their wake.

Roman didn't bother to detach her from him; instead he fell onto the bed with her on top of him.

He looked up at the woman who sat wantonly astride him… Given what he knew, *could she legitimately be called a woman*? He pushed aside the distracting question and indulged his senses fully in the delicious image—delicious curves, lush mouth and shiny take-me-now eyes.

Scarlet looked around her, her perplexed expression suggesting she didn't have the faintest idea how she'd come to be there.

The sultry, scared smile that she gave him made the ache in his groin almost unbearable. Still holding his eyes, she positioned a hand either side of his shoulders and leaned over him, her hair tumbling over her shoulders.

'What happened to your glasses?'

'Dark drawer time.' She kissed him, a long, deep, languid kiss.

'Pity, I liked them.'

'Liar,' she taunted huskily as she kissed her way up his neck.

'I had this fantasy about taking them off.'

'*Really?*' She blinked. 'You had fantasies about me?'

He laughed against her mouth. 'Oh, yes, Scarlet.' He gave a grunt of frustration as her luscious lips lifted from his. 'I've had several fantasies about you.'

'You could take something else off instead of the glasses,' she suggested huskily.

'I'd prefer to watch you do it.'

It was as she was unbuttoning the final button on her pyjama top that the wanton reality of what she was doing hit her. Roman, lying beneath her, his dark, intense gaze focused on her every move, saw the feelings of indecision reflected on her face.

'Let me,' he said, taking the white-knuckled fingers that were clutching the edges of the garment tightly together. Her lips parted to protest but their eyes touched and the resistance slid out of her. Still holding her eyes, he gently removed her stiff fingers.

The fabric parted.

Scarlet, overcome by self-consciousness, would have covered herself with her hands but he held them at her sides. The silence pulsated while his eyes feasted on the ivory perfection of her small pink-tipped breasts. He couldn't tear his eyes from the erotic sight; her body was bathed in a rosy flush of arousal that gave her skin a translucent quality.

'*Dio, cara,* you're so incredibly beautiful.' His voice, raw and needy, ached with sincerity.

Head inclined to one side, Scarlet searched his face, not quite confident enough to use the power she sensed she had over him. 'Truly?' she panted wonderingly.

Still holding her wrists, he turned over, pulling her beneath him. 'I never say things I don't mean,' he asserted imperiously.

Though she was only anchored beneath him for a moment before he slid off her and arranged his lean length beside her, it was long enough for her to know that that was where she wanted him. She wanted to feel the hot, heavy weight of his body on top of her. She wanted him to press her body into the softness of the mattress until it could sink no farther; she wanted him to sink into her.

Roman released her wrists but she made no attempt to move them from above her head. She turned her head towards him, and the sultry invitation glowing in her eyes wrenched a primitive groan from his throat before his mouth came crashing down hard and hungry on her lips.

Scarlet gave a soft moan of pleasure as he licked his way into her mouth, skilfully probing the sweet recesses. She welcomed the sensual demand of his lips and kissed him back enthusiastically, drowning in the pleasure as she felt his big hands on her body.

When his fingertips traced a delicate pathway along her straight, supple spine she shivered and stirred restively in his arms. The ripples of hot sensation went all the way to her curling toes. As his exploration shifted to her aching breasts the ripple became an avalanche.

He stroked and teased until her already painfully sensitised flesh felt as if it were on fire, *she* were on fire! She had never in her wildest fantasies come close to imagining the sort of blind, relentless hunger that gripped her at that moment.

When his fingers slid under the waistband of her pyjama bottoms she shivered hard and lifted her hips to help him slide them down her legs.

The air against her bare skin made her shiver. Scarlet opened her eyes and discovered he was propped up on one elbow looking down at her. He shifted his weight while he fought his way out of his damaged-beyond-repair shirt, not taking his dark liquid eyes from her as he casually flung the garment across the room.

Transfixed by the spectacle of perfectly toned muscle and deliciously smooth golden flesh, Scarlet gulped as her greedy eyes ate him up. She was weak with lust just looking at him. He was magnificent, perfect in every way, and the idea of touching that sleek, smooth body made her ache inside.

'You have a beautiful body.' There was a tremor of something close to reverence in his deep voice. 'So pale and perfect in every way.'

Scarlet, who had always compared herself with a beautiful sister, was extremely glad that beauty really did turn out to be in the eye of the beholder after all. But who would have guessed the beholder in question would turn out to be a man like Roman?

She rolled half onto her stomach and Roman's hot eyes zeroed in on the curve of her smooth peachy bottom. He inhaled slowly through flared nostrils when her small hand curved determinedly over him, he released the breath in a slow sibilant hiss as her fingers then tightened over him. Rhythmically she repeated the process again and again.

He was so much harder than she had imagined, feeling him pulse against her hand made the heavy, dragging sensation in the pit of her belly a hundred times more intense.

Her skin had acquired a sheen of moisture by the time he drew her tormenting hand from his body.

His eyes, dark and insolent, touched her face. 'Don't forget your place,' he instructed as he levered himself lightly from the bed.

Scarlet opened her mouth to protest and then saw he was unfastening his belt. The hot rush of desire that zapped through her left her literally panting for breath.

There was an electrified silence as he kicked aside his boxer shorts. Transfixed, she couldn't take her eyes off the hard contours of his taut, toned frame. There were no excess pounds to blur or disguise the perfect muscle definition of his upper body, flat belly and powerful thighs.

He was simply beautiful, a perfect bronzed statue come to life. She felt the prickle of emotional tears behind her eyelids as she feasted her eyes on him.

She was not conscious of moaning his name out loud, but she was conscious of the raw out-of-control light burning in his incredible eyes as he rejoined her. The skin-to-skin contact blasted the last shred of reason, of caution, from her head.

While he kissed her soft lips, deep searing kiss after deep searing kiss, she was all the time conscious of the hardness of his erection grinding into her belly. His skilful hands were moving over her sensitised body. She was equally driven to touch every inch of his smooth golden skin, explore every centimetre of the taut, silky surface.

The air was filled with gasps, hoarse whimpers of pleasure and muted moans.

Ultra receptive to his skilful touch, she writhed and twisted when his hands cupped her breasts; she grabbed his head and cried out when his tongue lashed teasingly across the tight, engorged peaks.

He laughed when she brokenly claimed to be dying—she was only half joking.

'Try and hold on a little longer,' he instructed as he mercilessly began to lick his way down the softness of her quivering belly. She stiffened when his exploration reached the soft fuzz at the apex of her legs.

'Relax, *cara*,' he breathed into her ear.

'But…'

It wasn't his kiss but the unexpected tenderness in his eyes that stilled her protest.

'Don't think, let yourself feel. That's it,' he approved throatily as she pushed against his fingers with a sigh.

'I don't know what I'm doing…in theory I know, but…'

'I know what I'm doing.'

He did.

Because he had had a lot of practice… *He's right, I shouldn't think.*

'And you're not doing so badly, *cara*. Oh, my God, you're so tight,' he breathed hoarsely as he slid a finger inside her.

'That's…*oh, my God*…! Please, Roman, please…'

A considerable amount of pleading and even more indescribable pleasure later, he pulled her knees up and settled between her legs. A shiver of voluptuous anticipation slid through her as she felt the probing pressure of his hard silkiness against the very core of her.

No pain, not really, just pressure and then the mind-expanding miracle of being filled.

He was on top of her and inside her and everything that was happening had a feeling of rightness about it.

That was her last conscious thought as he began to move and the pressure inside her started to build. The first ripples of her orgasm wrenched a deep moan from her parted lips.

I *screamed*! The shocking memory of the feral scream as her orgasm had peaked flashed through her head.

Roman felt the warm body pressed close to him tense. 'Is something wrong?' he asked, stroking the damp hair from her face.

'Nothing,' Scarlet sighed, relaxing back into arms that closed tightly around her.

What could be wrong? She was where she wanted to be. Things like him not loving her could wait until the morning.

It was actually around two in the morning when the shrill ring of the phone roused her. She rubbed her eyes and sleepily reached out only to find there was a large naked male in the way.

She sat bolt upright, suddenly very wide awake. Not daring to look at the shadowy shape in the bed beside her. Carefully she edged her body away from his, difficult in such a narrow bed, and reached over him for the phone.

'Hello…'

'Firstly, don't panic, Sam is fine. Fast asleep, actually.' Tom Bradley went on to explain that it was their son who was unwell. The doctor had been called and he was off to the hospital with suspected appendicitis.

Scarlet expressed her heartfelt sympathy. 'Poor Nancy. How is she?'

'Tearful,' her husband admitted. 'I've told her that kids bounce back but she doesn't cope well with illness.'

Scarlet could hear the stress in his voice. 'So you'd like me to pick Sam up.'

'Well, that's up to you, the au pair is here and he's asleep, but…'

'I'll pick him up now,' Scarlet said, manoeuvring herself out of the bed as she spoke. 'You'll be at the hospital by the time I get there?'

'We're off now.'

'I'm sure he'll be fine, but good luck anyway,' she said before hanging up.

She was halfway across the room when the bedside light was switched on. She froze like an animal caught in the headlights of the car.

'Has something happened to Sam?'

Well, she couldn't complain that he didn't have his priorities right. A naked woman standing less then five feet away and his first thoughts were for his son…as it should be, and very commendable, but she wouldn't have minded being a *slight* distraction.

'Sam's fine.' She walked to the chest of drawers trying to act as if she weren't desperately self-conscious. 'It's his friend from the sleep-over who has suspected appendicitis. That was his dad, Tom Bradley, just now, the *Tom Bradley* you've *never* met,' she inserted drily.

'I'm going to pick Sam up. Could you call me a taxi, please?' She pulled a fresh set of undies from the drawer and stepped into the knickers.

On the whole, she thought she had carried off the entire I'm-perfectly-happy-with-my-body thing really well.

'Don't be stupid, I'll take you.' She heard the creak of bed springs as he got out of bed.

'That's really not necessary,' she started, and froze as she felt his fingers brush her bare back.

'Let me,' he said, snapping the bra catch she had been clumsily trying to fasten first time. She didn't see how he could have failed to feel the shiver that rippled through her body.

'Thank you,' she said huskily. 'Sorry I woke you.' She could no longer avoid looking at him.

'You didn't wake me. I haven't been asleep.'

Unlike her, Roman did not possess any inhibitions about nakedness. Her eyes slid of their own volition down his body and made the discovery that made her blush.

'There will be other mornings,' he promised.

Blushing even more fierily, she looked away and snatched up a shirt that was draped over the back of a chair. 'No,' she contradicted huskily, 'there won't be other mornings.'

Roman's eyes narrowed as she turned her back but he didn't comment on her statement. Any idea she had that he had accepted or not noticed what she'd said was laid to rest when she was safely belted into the passenger seat of his silver Jaguar.

The streets were virtually deserted as he drove through the silent city.

'Why won't there be any other mornings?'

'It was marvellous and so were you, if that's what's worrying you.' Her attempt at light laughter emerged as a croak.

'It wasn't. I'm well aware that what happened between us was special, which is why you're not making sense.'

It was hard to keep her focus when he said 'special' in that sexy, throaty way, but Scarlet knew she had to. He was a passionate, highly sexed man and the chemistry was intense between them, but how soon before she began to see his picture in the newspapers with other women?

Worse still, would she turn into the woman he went back to when there was nothing better on offer? *The sure thing.*

She hadn't wanted to get into this now, but she realised that discussing it while he had to keep his eyes on the road and his hands on the steering wheel was actually not such a bad idea.

'I can't sleep with you again because it wouldn't be good for Sam. He can't see us as a couple and then not—children need continuity. But don't worry, we can work out a schedule for you to visit with him. Though I'd prefer you wait a little while before you have him for the weekend or anything.'

'I'm sure if you dig really deep there is some logic there somewhere.' The amusement in his voice sounded pretty strained as he added heavily, 'Damned if I can find it, though.' The furrows on his brow deepened. 'What has Sam to do with you sleeping with me? Or, for that matter, you *not* sleeping with me?'

'Well, you did imply that it would be convenient if you could sleep over.'

His jaw tightened by several notches. 'I would want to make love to you if there was no Sam. Even in the incredibly ugly glasses I wanted to make love to you. It's called chemistry, *cara*!' he yelled. 'There is a Sam, though, and you can't ignore the fact that us being together will be a good thing for him.'

'When you say "together", that's not what you really mean.' Together to her meant exclusive, it meant commitment, it meant, in an ideal world, love.

'I take it you're going to tell me what I mean.'

The sardonic edge in his voice made her lips compress.

'If you had turned up and found the woman bringing up your child had a string of casual lovers move in with her you'd have been the first to hit the ceiling.'

'That's a totally different thing,' he responded immediately.

'In what way?'

He didn't reply, but a sneaky sideways look told her he was looking explosively angry. Again she was glad he was driving—this way he couldn't throttle her or, much more dangerous, kiss her.

'It would just confuse Sam, Roman. He needs things clearly defined. You can't jeopardise your relationship with him for casual sex.'

'I thought you didn't do casual sex.'

'So did I,' she admitted, her unhappiness showing. She dragged a hand through her hair. 'Obviously you are going to be a part of Sam's life for a long time, and therefore mine.'

'I can see how happy that makes you.'

She glared at his perfect profile. 'This is serious.'

A flash of dark annoyance crossed his taut face. 'I am serious,' he rebutted grimly.

'This is about putting a child's needs first.'

The car slowed at a set of lights and he turned his head. 'A parent's life sounds fun: self-sacrifice and no sex.'

'You're taking what I'm saying out of context and you know it,' she accused. 'Sex within a stable relationship is fine.'

The car behind sounded its horn and Roman cursed softly under his breath as he saw the lights had turned green. 'I'm not surprised you were a damned virgin if you want a marriage proposal before you accept a dinner date,' he observed cuttingly as he pulled away.

He cast a quick sideways glance at her white stricken face and turned his attention back to the road ahead. A few yards farther down the road he released a flood of low impassioned Italian, before heaving a deep sigh.

'Fine, have your schedule, keep me at arm's length. I'll keep my distance for as long as you want me to.'

Scarlet nodded, having decided that on balance it was simpler to pretend she hadn't noticed his get-out clause.

Roman appeared oblivious to the awkward silence that developed and she was relieved when a few minutes later they reached the gate to the Bradley house.

'This is it.'

As they drew up outside the front of the house beside a

BMW and a big four-wheel drive Scarlet unfastened her seat belt.

'Do you want me to wait here?'

She sent him a startled look. 'Not unless you prefer not to come in.'

'I don't want to alarm him. I'm a stranger.'

He was nervous! She felt every kind of insensitive idiot for not realising sooner.

'You're not a stranger, Roman, you're his dad.' She wanted to wrap her arms around him.

Their eyes met and for a moment he stared at her, then he smiled and her heart began to thud. She jumped out of the car before she did something really stupid.

The au pair had obviously been waiting for them.

'Sam's asleep.' Scarlet saw the girl's eyes widen as Roman joined her. It amused her—well, actually, it annoyed her—that as far as the girl was concerned she had become invisible. 'If you'd like to come in, I'll show you the way.'

She went as far as the door of the bedroom and, with a nod, left them. 'I'll be downstairs if you want me.' This was said with a wistful glance at Roman, who, to give him his due, seemed totally oblivious to the effect he had.

Sam was fast asleep, his cherubic face flushed rosily with sleep.

The awed expression on Roman's face as he looked down at the child brought a lump to her throat. Scarlet handed him the fleecy blanket she had brought with her.

'Wrap him up in this, will you? It's his favourite blanket.'

'You want me to carry him?'

To see the ultra-confident Roman look nervous rung her tender heart. 'Yes, please.'

'If he wakes up and sees me...'

She smiled encouragingly. 'Sam doesn't wake easily.'

Sam did wake. He opened his eyes and looked up into the face of the man who was carrying him. He gave a sleepy frown.

'Did you bring me a football?'

'Next time,' Roman promised.

Sam smiled and closed his eyes. 'Good,' he said as he snuggled down into the big man's arms.

Roman shook his head. His eyes were shining; he looked as though someone had just given him the winning Lotto ticket. 'He remembered me.'

There was an emotional lump in her throat that made her voice thick. 'You're not an easy man to forget,' she said, turning away before he saw that she was crying.

CHAPTER TWELVE

SCARLET caught sight of his reflection in the steamy window: a tall man, his lean, long frame filled the doorway. She might only have been feasting her eyes on a reflection, but it didn't stop her receiving the same shocking jolt of sexual longing she always did when he appeared—sleek and sexy and totally out of place, not just in her kitchen, but her life.

Maybe he won't be a presence for much longer?

The prospect of Roman vanishing from their lives should have made her happy. Wasn't it what she'd been praying for right from the start? She felt many things but happiness wasn't one of them.

Since he'd pushed his way into her life she was permanently stressed and edgy. Though she had to admit Roman's behaviour had been impeccable. He had not even raised an eyebrow when she had produced the promised schedule, though when she'd pinned it to the notice-board in the kitchen he hadn't been able to resist a comment about her colour coding.

Three weeks into the arrangement it was hard to remember when he hadn't been a part of Sam's life.

He wasn't the problem; she was!

It had been three days since his last visit. On that visit he'd had a free afternoon and it had been agreed that he would take Sam for a walk in the park. The weather had been perfect, unlike Sam's mood. The toddler had been tired, which always made him cranky, and the fact she hadn't let him watch a programme on the television that looked unsuitable to her had not improved matters.

Roman had not seen his son in this mood before. He had looked uncharacteristically helpless when the toddler had struggled and thrown himself around when he had tried to put his coat on. Acting like a three-year-old who hadn't got his own way, Sam hadn't even looked at the gift Roman had brought for him.

Roman might be intolerant and short-tempered in his dealings with her, but Scarlet had to admit that with Sam he displayed a limitless supply of patience. When, despite his best efforts, the child had remained stubbornly cranky, Scarlet had finally taken pity on the inexperienced father— in truth she had found the usually totally self-possessed and poised playboy looking helpless dangerously appealing.

'I'll come, if you'd like. I could do with some fresh air,' she heard herself offer.

Of course she ought to have let him trail Sam around the park on his own; that would have brought home big time to him that taking care of a young child was not all ice cream and fun games.

Even with her along to retrieve the toy that Sam deliberately threw from the pushchair every few yards the park thing wasn't a raving success. Though it was worth going just to see how horrified Roman looked as he pushed a child who was having a tantrum through town.

'What's wrong with him?' he asked Scarlet in a hushed undertone. 'Is he ill?'

She shook her head. She was amused by his harassed question but, not being a fool, hid the fact. 'Not even possessed by a demon,' she told him cheerfully. 'He's tired, that's all. A nap and he'll be fine. He's fighting sleep—he doesn't want to give in,' she explained knowledgeably.

'He's also fighting me. People are staring.'

Scarlet looked at his heartbreakingly perfect profile. 'You ought to be used to that,' she told him drily.

Despite his discomfort, Roman ironically didn't show any sign of self-consciousness about being the cynosure of curious eyes when a few minutes later he leapt to his son's defence.

She recalled the event with a wry smile. The passer-by who loudly offered the opinion that what that child needed was a firm hand and or good slap got more than he had bargained for when confronted by an icily irate father.

Roman said, in a voice that made Scarlet shiver, that anyone who hit a child in anger was a coward and a bully at the very least. And anyone who hit *his* child would find him or herself regretting the action for the rest of their natural life!

The man's face was a picture.

Since the last visit, Roman had been meant to come around the previous day, but he had cancelled at the last minute. As she had explained to Sam that his daddy wouldn't be coming after all she had wondered whether after the trip in the park he was having second thoughts about the joys of fatherhood.

She didn't turn around immediately even though she could feel his dark eyes drilling into her back. Waiting for her pulse rate to slow to a canter, she continued to dry the dishes stacked on the draining-board as though achieving a shiny finish on the crockery were something she had always wanted to dedicate her life to.

'Had we arranged for you to come over this evening?' she asked, holding a polished glass up to the light to check for smudges.

'I must have lost my schedule,' he returned with an equal amount of irony.

'There's no need to be facetious,' she snapped. 'You can't

just barge in here whenever it suits you. I have a life of my own.'

'The jury is still out on that one.'

Scarlet bit back a retort to this jibe. 'This is only going to work if you accept I have a right to my privacy...'

'To dry dishes? Yes, I can see that it's a uniquely private moment between a plate and a woman. I'm so sorry I intruded.'

Scarlet, the tea towel still clutched in her white-knuckled fingers, spun around, her eyes flashing green. 'You can laugh, but I doubt if you'd like it if I dropped in at your office or home any time I felt like it.'

'And do you feel like dropping in on me often?'

Scarlet refused to drop her eyes in face of the glittering challenge she saw in his. 'All the time,' she drawled sarcastically, 'but so far I'm keeping my impulses under control.'

God knew how long that would last. He looked incredibly gorgeous tonight in a grey designer tee shirt and jeans.

His eyes dropped and lingered on the lush contours of her slightly parted lips. Scarlet felt the predictable debilitating weakness spread through her body. She had no doubt at all that his action was cynically deliberate and indicated nothing more than the fact he got some twisted enjoyment out of seeing her get confused, but she was unable not to react to it.

'Not on my account—*I'm* all for following your natural instincts,' Roman said. Scarlet felt the heat unfurl low in her belly and fought the insidious effects of his warm honey-eyed voice.

'I'm not interested in your natural instincts except when they result in you letting Sam down.' Anger at her own weakness made her voice harsh. 'Rule number one,' she outlined coldly, 'is you don't make promises to Sam you can't keep. I won't have him disappointed because you had a better offer!' she flared contemptuously.

Roman's chin went up to a haughty angle, his nostrils flared, but the signalled anger didn't arrive. Instead his hard boned features relaxed into a speculative expression as he studied her face with a curiosity that rang alarm bells in her head.

'Is this really about *Sam's* disappointment?'

'Of course.'

'Or are you jealous that I spent the evening with someone else?' he suggested silkily. 'Did you miss me?'

Scarlet swallowed. 'In your dreams!'

'Yes, just lately you are, and the fact is I'd much prefer to have you in my bed,' he acknowledged, his voice roughened with frustration. 'And I'm damned sure you'd like to be there. The question is, why aren't you?'

'I slept with you once.'

'It hadn't slipped my memory.'

His sardonic interruption brought a militant gleam to her eyes. 'And you know perfectly well why it's a bad idea, we've been through all that.'

'Remind me.' His eyes were as hard and unforgiving as slate as they drilled into her.

'I can see you're in a mood…'

His head went back, exposing the strong brown line of his throat, and he gave a derisive snort. 'And you wonder why?'

'I think you're just being awkward for the sake of it!' she accused.

'I can do awkward, but this isn't it.' His dark eyes flashed angrily. 'Where is Sam?'

'Upstairs in number ten playing with Tessa, Isobel's little girl.'

'The woman upstairs?'

Scarlet nodded. 'Her little girl is about Sam's age—they get on really well.'

'That's convenient.'

'Are you suggesting that it's handy for me to have someone to dump Sam on?'

'*No.*' Without Roman raising his voice the softly spoken denial stilled the angry words spilling from her. 'That's not what I'm suggesting.'

Scarlet's shoulders relaxed but the frown that furrowed her smooth brow remained. 'But you are suggesting something?' she speculated shrewdly.

He shrugged and smiled back at her in that infuriatingly enigmatic way he had.

'I think this weekend might be a good time for a trip to Ireland.'

Very slowly Scarlet finished wiping the mug in her hand and replaced it on the counter. 'Have a nice time,' she said in a voice that was carefully devoid of all expression. *My God, I'm going to miss him!* The recognition of how much was a shock. 'I might invite Isobel over for tea,' she added brightly. 'Sam gets on well with her little girl.'

'So you said.'

'Sorry if I'm boring you,' she returned childishly.

'Scarlet, I'm not going to Ireland alone.'

Stupid me, of course he isn't. With horror she recognised the sickening feeling that stabbed through her as jealousy, which was stupid; she had wanted it this way. Was that why he was spelling it out? Had he picked up before she had on the possessive feelings she was developing…?

'Anyone I know?' she asked casually.

'You and Sam. My father would like to meet you both.'

Scarlet's blinked. 'Me and Sam?' she echoed. 'I don't understand.'

'Neither do I,' he remarked cryptically before taking her

chin in his hand and tilting her face up towards him. The dark spiky lashes lifted off her cheek and big almond-shaped eyes that he knew could vary in shade quite dramatically stared back up at him.

'I'd like you and Sam to come home with me to Ireland,' he repeated patiently. His brows lifted and he gave a lop-sided grin and exasperation slipped into his voice as he asked, 'Who the hell did you think I was going to take home to meet my parents?'

An image of several beauties his name had been linked with flashed through her mind as she shook her head. 'I really don't care.' She moved her head and his light touch fell away.

'Then what do you care about?'

The soft question had a curious driven quality to it that brought her eyes back to his face.

I could look at that face for ever and never get tired of looking. 'The fact that no matter what you promise the mo-ment my back is turned you're there again organising my life, Sam's life, and taking over!' she accused hoarsely.

'You're being ridiculous,' Roman contended, looking genuinely bewildered by her accusation.

'Fine, so you don't expect us to come with you just like that!' She clicked her fingers but the dampness on her skin prevented the action producing a satisfying crack.

Roman clicked his tongue and shook his dark head form side to side. 'Not like that, like this,' he said, taking her empty hand and arranging her thumb and forefinger in the required position. 'It's all in the tension.'

Of that there was plenty!

His touch was light, clinical almost, but the softest touch from him sent every nerve ending in her body awake and screaming for more. A terrible surge of longing welled up in her; it was so intense that she could feel it in her bones.

Their eyes connected and a voluptuous shiver ran all the way to her toes.

Angrily she snatched her hand away and rubbed it up and down against her thigh. Her eyes were wary and fiery as she avoided direct eye contact.

'It didn't occur to you it would have been a nice gesture to *ask* not *inform*?'

The impatience in Roman's face visibly increased as she spoke. 'Or I could have been really subtle and let you think it was your idea all along?' he suggested.

'Only you could call manipulative straightforward.' She shook her head incredulously—he really was a one-off. 'I don't suppose that it occurred to you that I might have made other plans, did it? No,' she added without giving him an opening to respond. 'It wouldn't, because you never consider anyone else but yourself!' she declared angrily.

Roman's eyes lifted. They were smouldering.

'I didn't consider that you'd made plans because as far as I can see you don't have a social life.'

'Not one like yours, certainly.'

'Since Sam was born your life has revolved around him. Can you deny that?'

'Are you saying I smother him?'

'I'd say the possibility of you wearing yourself to a shadow trying to be the perfect mother is a more likely scenario.'

Scarlet threw a hand up. 'You've been a father, what? Five minutes, and you're telling me what I'm doing wrong.'

He opened his mouth to deliver a cutting rejoinder and his gaze settled on her face. Suddenly the anger drained out of him. She looked so tired, he thought, looking at the purplish bruises under her eyes. He experienced a wave of protective tenderness of shocking intensity.

'Consider yourself asked.'

Scarlet looked at him blankly. 'What?'

'I'm *asking* if you and Sam will come to Ireland with me this weekend.'

'It's quite impossible. A trip like that will muck up Sam's routine and I have work on Monday.'

'You're the impossible one!' he flung, literally grinding his teeth in frustration. 'Sam's routine is not engraved in stone. I thought you said it was important with a child to be flexible?'

'This wasn't what I was talking about.'

'Now there's a surprise.' The muscles in his taut jaw tightened another notch. 'As for work, you have four weeks' holiday to take before the end of next month and I happen to know there won't be any objection to you taking some of it next week.'

'And you'd know that because?'

'It always pays to think ahead,' he drawled, seemingly unaffected by the tremble of anger in her voice.

'I can't believe you went behind my back,' she choked. 'How *dare* you interfere in my life this way? This is exactly what I was talking about. I'm not some puppet you can manipulate.'

'How much simpler life would be,' he drawled.

Scarlet shot him a furious glance. 'Well, there's absolutely no way we're coming now. What…what's that?' she said, stopping mid-sentence to stare suspiciously at the newspaper he had drawn from his pocket and thrown on the worktop.

'You'll find the relevant article on page two. It's an evening edition. I think we'll make the front page tomorrow morning. What you read there might make you reconsider your decision. I don't think London is going to be a very comfortable place for you.'

As he spoke his eyes were trained on Scarlet, who was turning the page with considerable trepidation.

'I feel sick!' she declared when the half-page picture headlined DOMESTIC BLISS…? jumped out at her. It was a cosy domestic scene. Roman was manoeuvring Sam's pushchair up a pavement in the park. Sam himself was asleep, his head lolling to one side. Scarlet, her head turned slightly away from the camera, was looking up at Roman and smiling.

'They didn't catch my good side, but you look cute.'

'How can you joke about this?' Scarlet demanded, raising reproachful shell-shocked eyes to his face. She shook her head and protested in a dazed tone, 'We're not going to go public yet.'

'I think we just have.' Roman sounded remarkably philosophical about it. Although you're still the mystery brunette and they've stopped short of saying that Sam is my son, I think it's significant that there are five references to the uncanny resemblance.'

'You didn't arrange this, did you?'

He sucked in his breath audibly. 'No, I did not. I'm pretty sure it was your neighbour upstairs who did that.'

'Isobel wouldn't do that!' she gasped, appalled. 'She's my friend.'

'One who you've known for what? A week?'

'That's only three weeks less than I've known you and you expect me to trust you?'

'And you'd prefer that I was the bad guy. I get your sister pregnant, but it's you who have to be there to hold her hand while she's dying and bring up my son when she's gone. This record is not one to inspire confidence or trust, I can see that, but right now I am here and all I want is to get to know my son.'

'I don't blame you for what happened to Abby.'

'Why the hell not? If the positions were reversed I would.'

Scarlet looked around for something else to dry; this was a subject she didn't want to get into.

With an exasperated grunt Roman snatched the tea towel from her fingers and spun her around to face him.

'Your friend might have nothing to do with this, but when I met her she seemed very interested in my relationship with Sam and you.'

'I didn't know you'd met her.'

'The other day when I was arriving she just happened to be coming out her door and you said yourself that Isobel was hard up for cash. Hasn't her husband lost his job?'

'You're saying she wasn't my friend, she was just using me?' Distress roughened her voice.

'I'm sure she liked you too, but maybe she saw a way to make some money and the temptation was too great to resist. It's incredible how flexible your principles can become when you've no money for the rent.'

'You don't even sound angry!' she gasped, raising tear-filled eyes to his face.

'Do you think nobody who said they were my friend has ever done the dirty on me?' he asked.

'It's awful. No wonder you're so horribly cynical,' she observed. 'Not,' she added with a sniff, 'that I'm going to condemn someone without proof.'

'Quite right, I'm just pointing out a possibility.'

He scanned her ivory-pale face and walked over to the fridge and withdrew a half-open bottle of wine from the door. He filled a glass and wrapped her stiff fingers around it. 'You're in shock and it should be brandy, but I don't suppose you keep any spirits.'

'I have no secrets from you,' she bit back sardonically through chattering teeth.

'Drink the lot,' he insisted, standing over her to make sure she did as he ordered. 'Feel any better?'

'No, just dizzy.' She lifted her eyes to his. 'What are we going to do?'

'We are going to do nothing. We are not going to respond when journalists ask us—'

'But what if—?'

He shook his head. 'We do not respond,' he told her flatly. 'Listen, I know you're not used to handling the media, which is why I thought a few days of time out in Ireland might be a good idea.'

'Don't you mean hiding…running away?'

'No, I don't mean hiding or running away.'

'But that's what it amounts to,' she objected with a frown.

'You'd prefer to be here when the telephone starts ringing or you wake up to find them camping on your doorstep?'

A shudder of revulsion ran through Scarlet at the image his words conjured up. She was an intensely private person; the idea of having her face and name the object of specu- lation was abhorrent. 'Is that going to happen?' she asked fearfully.

'You'll have a camera lens trained on every window,' he predicted. He looked around the tiny room. 'And this flat could not offer less protection.'

'My entire life can't change because of a silly story in a newspaper,' she protested, her voice rising shrilly. 'Perhaps I should go and stay with a friend?' she suggested.

'You could, if you want to lay them open to the same intrusive media invasion,' he agreed. 'Or you could come with me to Ireland.'

'You think they'll have lost interest in the story by the time we get back?' she suggested hopefully. 'I mean, it's bound to die a natural death really, isn't it, if I go away for a while?'

There was a moment's silence before his dark lashes lifted and he looked directly at her. 'Anything is possible.'

His cagey response didn't sound too comforting to Scarlet. 'But if they want a story or pictures they could follow us to Ireland. Where do you register on the scale of newsworthy?' she demanded. 'Would they follow you to Ireland?'

'Sorry they would, but it wouldn't do them much good. The house is set in the middle of a couple of thousand acres, part of it heavily forested, which means even fly-overs by helicopter are unproductive.

'It's an added plus factor that the neighbours are as unfriendly to the press as the geography. Sometimes,' he mused, 'friends are more effective than a million pounds' worth of security, not that we haven't invested in some of that of late,' he added drily.

'Your stalker?'

'I suppose you read about that.'

'No, your mother mentioned something about it and I've seen the scar, remember?' she added huskily. Her fingertips tingled as she recalled running her fingers along the ridge of scar tissue that stood out pale against his smooth dark skin. Shocking, sensual heat washed over her until she was engulfed from head to toe.

Their eyes touched and locked. *'I remember.'*

A soft, sibilant hiss issued from his lips at the same moment a deep shudder rippled through her body. The sexual tension fed on the electricity that passed between them and became a palpable presence in the room.

Scarlet knew that a gigantic black hole had opened up at her feet and, God, did she want to step into it! Every fibre in her body told her to let go, what the hell? How could this be wrong when it felt so good? From somewhere she dredged up the will-power to cling to the fragments of her self-control.

'It must have been a terrible experience.' Her voice sounded high and brittle to her own critical ears. 'Is she…the woman…?'

'In a psychiatric unit, but making good progress by all accounts. Hopefully she'll be well enough to be released later this year.'

Despite her best intentions this comment brought Scarlet's attention back to his face. If it weren't for the thin line of feverish colour that focused the eye on his high cheekbones she might have thought she had imagined that moment of mutual lust. Now she knew that she hadn't imagined anything—his desire was still there, raw and dangerous…but, worse still, deeply exciting.

Dear God, girl, show a bit of control.

'I don't think I'd be hoping for that in your shoes,' she admitted huskily. The knowledge that give or take a few inches he could have died at the hands of the crazy woman sent a chill through her.

'She was sick, people get sick…'

'But she nearly—'

'But she didn't,' he cut in firmly. 'If we spent our lives worrying about what could have happened we'd never get out of bed in the morning.'

'If we did come with you when we came back the press would still be waiting?'

Roman nodded.

'Wouldn't it be better to get it all over with rather than postpone the inevitable?' The look she directed up at him did not contain the same bold fearlessness of her suggestion.

'You seem pretty adept at avoiding the inevitable,' Roman observed drily. He watched the give-away warm colour bloom on her pale cheeks and smiled.

'Please try and concentrate,' she rebuked.

'It's very hard when you're standing there looking so luscious.'

His voice might have contained a teasing note but there was nothing light-hearted about the raw, needy expression in the eyes that moved in a compulsive fashion over her slender body.

'Don't be silly!' Scarlet found it incredible that someone who had escorted some of the most glamorous women in the country could look at her wearing her oldest jeans and a washed out tee shirt, with no make-up and her hair tied back in a pony-tail, and feel desire.

While her brain told her that it was impossible for him to feel that way about her, her eyes told her differently. Her body—well, actually her body had an agenda of its own. Her body wanted to get as close as possible to this man.

God knew where it came from, but somehow she found the strength not to throw herself at him.

'I need you to be serious for a moment.'

An expression of regret formed on Roman's face as he examined her pale features. She was trying to put a brave face on it in a typically Scarlet way.

He would have given a lot to offer the reassurance she was obviously seeking from him. It frustrated the hell out of him that the matter had been taken out of his hands, but he knew that he would be doing her no favours if he pretended the problem was going to go away.

'I mean, *obviously* I'm not going to go out of my way to provide photo opportunities for these people, but isn't it a cop-out to put your life on hold because of a couple of men with cameras?'

'It's not going to be a couple of men with cameras,' he told her as gently as he could. 'There are going to be a horde of them, a siege. Journos are going to be phoning you offering you money for a chance to tell your side of the story, shoving notes under your front door when you don't answer...'

Scarlet listened to him, growing paler and paler. She held up her hand. 'Don't!' she pleaded. Her lower lip wobbled as a sob rose in her throat. 'Why is this happening?' she wailed. 'It's not fair.' A sigh shuddered through her as Roman's arms drew her against him and then closed around her.

She knew at some level that the safety his arms offered was an illusion, but it didn't actually seem to matter. What mattered was it felt warm and good.

'I know it's not fair,' she heard him murmur into her hair. 'It will pass, I promise, it will pass.' His hand ran down the curve of her back and with a sigh she snuggled a little closer.

She sensed the tension in his lean body as he drew slightly back from her and she lifted a tear-stained face in enquiry.

With a fierce tenderness that stopped her heart in its tracks Roman ran a finger down the curve of her cheek, then smoothed the hair back from her brow.

'So you'll come to Ireland with me.'

Scarlet's heart was beating very hard. 'Right now I'd go anywhere with you,' she confided huskily.

'Does that include to bed?'

'Especially there.'

With a soft cry she walked into his open arms.

CHAPTER THIRTEEN

'WHEN you said you were phobic about flying why didn't you also mention that you get seasick?' Roman asked as Scarlet emerged from the ladies' loo where she had spent ninety per cent of the journey so far.

Scarlet shot him a look of intense dislike, and grabbed the back of the seat to steady herself before she lowered herself on the seat beside the sleeping toddler.

'But this feels like a force-ten gale,' she declared, averting her eyes from the grey heaving waves visible through the window. 'I wish I could sit outside—I always feel better outside. Why isn't there a deck?' she complained querulously.

Roman laughed. 'Do you prefer a conventional ferry with a deck or this fast ferry which halves the crossing time?'

She nodded glumly. 'I see your point.'

'And for the record there isn't a wave to be seen—it's as calm as a millpond. I've crossed when—'

Scarlet lifted a hand to her forehead. 'Spare me the stories of your heroics, please?' she begged sourly. 'I'm surprised you've ever been on a ferry.'

'I did some island hopping when I was a student, but, no, this isn't my preferred mode of transport.' It had taken him ten minutes to convince Alice he was serious when he'd asked her to book three tickets on a ferry across the Irish Sea.

'Sorry you're slumming it on my account.'

'It's been a revelation,' he assured her drily.

'You're such a snob.'

'I did crew on a yacht in a cross-Atlantic race once.'

'I suppose you won?'

'No, we came last.'

'How very human of you,' she snapped with bitchy relish.

She closed her eyes. There was no question that she could ever form any sort of meaningful relationship with someone who ate a full English breakfast on board a boat. She opened one eye. 'Thank you for looking after Sam.'

'A pleasure. Perhaps I should have booked us into a hotel overnight before the drive.'

'No, I'll be fine once I'm on land that doesn't move,' she promised him.

Roman considered her pallid complexion but kept his doubts to himself. 'You *really* prefer this to flying?'

'I've never actually flown,' she confided.

'Never?'

The amazement from someone who considered getting on a plane the same way most people thought of getting in a cab brought a wan smile to her lips.

'I tried it once but the stuff the doctor prescribed didn't mix too well with the whisky I drank in the bar before I boarded. I passed out and they had to stretcher me out. Abby was so embarrassed,' she recalled, 'that she pretended she didn't know me.'

'So you got left at home?'

Something in his voice brought her puzzled scrutiny to his face. 'I didn't actually mind. I'm not really a lazing-on-a-beach sort of person.'

'Shopaholic or culture vulture?'

'There are some places I would like to see one day,' she admitted, covering her mouth to conceal a wide yawn. 'Rome, Paris...you know...maybe when Sam is older.'

The hand that brushed the hair from her forehead made her start.

'You're tired.'

She sensed activity to her right just a split second before Roman leapt up from his seat.

She turned in time to see Roman pull a middle aged man who was slumped in his seat down onto the floor. He proceeded to loosen the man's collar and felt at his neck for a pulse before Scarlet's brain had registered what was going on.

The woman who had been sitting beside the unconscious—*please, God, let him be alive*—man began to scream and people began to shout. It said something for Roman's natural air of command that when he lifted his hand to indicate he needed silence, just before he placed his ear to the man's chest, a hush fell.

He straightened up and struck the man with some force on his chest. He then tilted the man's head back and pinched his nose. 'Anybody here know CPR?' he asked in the same non-urgent way he'd done everything else. As he bent to breathe into the man's mouth a scruffy-looking teenager counted him out before applying compressions to the man's chest in an expert way.

They continued this until two members of staff took over from them. Another member of staff politely asked the passengers sitting in the near vicinity to move. Scarlet was struggling to transfer herself and a very sleepy Sam to another part of the boat when Roman appeared at her side.

'Come on up here, champ,' he said, casually lifting Sam up one-handed. 'Give this to me,' he added, indicating the holdall she had looped over her shoulder.

'I can manage.' He treated her to one of his trade-mark ironic looks—the ones that made her feel incredibly childish—and she handed it over with a sigh.

'This weighs a ton. I don't know why women need to cart so much junk around with them.'

Scarlet couldn't let this sexist criticism pass. 'For your information, virtually nothing in there is mine. Sam doesn't travel light. There are the changes of clothes—'

'*Changes*—? You've got more than one set in there?'

'You don't know many three-year-olds, do you, Roman?' she observed, dealing him a superior look. 'Then there's the waterproof in case it rains and drinks…*obviously*. A packed lunch because he's a bit of a fussy eater and some crayons and a—'

A smile tugged at the corners of Roman's mobile lips as he listened to her narrate the contents. 'All right, I get the picture.'

Having secured them alternative seats, he turned to Scarlet, his dark eyes sweeping assessingly over her pale features. 'How are you feeling?'

'Fine.'

He looked less than convinced. 'I admire your stoical attitude—' in Scarlet's opinion his attitude suggested exasperation rather than admiration '—but only this morning I thought turning green was a figure of speech. A boat journey with you has taught me otherwise.'

'That poor man tends to put seasickness into proportion.' She gave a quick glance at Sam and saw he was happily preoccupied. Fortunately he had slept right through the crisis. 'How…how is he? He's not…?' She hardly dared ask.

'He started breathing.'

Scarlet gave a noisy sigh of relief. 'Well thank goodness for that!'

'He's hardly out of the woods yet,' Roman warned.

Scarlet shook her head in agreement. 'But he has a chance, thanks to you,' she added warmly.

'Basic first aid is all.' Roman seemed inclined to make light of his contribution. 'If I hadn't got there first someone else would have done what was needed. The ferry company staff are pretty well equipped to cope until the helicopter arrives.'

'They're going to air-lift him to hospital? Is that possible while we're at sea?'

Roman nodded. 'The bad news is it involves stopping the engine so they can winch him off. I'm afraid this is going to add another half hour at least to the journey.'

Scarlet took a deep breath. 'Right…' Under the circumstances she could hardly complain, even though being on the boat for a minute longer than necessary made her want to weep.

She felt his eyes on her face and lifted her chin. 'Trust you to be a hero,' she condemned with a teasing little grimace.

An amazed laugh was drawn from her throat. 'I'm embarrassing you, aren't I?' It was ironic—she tried her best to discompose him and failed miserably, when all she had to do apparently was say something nice about him.

'Would you like something to eat?'

Scarlet closed her eyes and released a weak groan. 'You really are a horrible man with no heart, you know that, don't you?'

'I'm hurt.'

Even with her eyes closed she could hear the grin in his voice. 'I live in hope.'

'I'm just trying to take your mind off it.' He had thought of other methods but these might have got him arrested in a public place.

'If you're about to suggest that it's all in my mind and all I need is positive thinking, I'll kill you. Also you are totally wrong—it's all in my inner ear; it's a balance thing.' Her eyes flickered open and a deep shudder ran all the way to her toes at a touch of warm air against her sensitive earlobe.

Roman, his hand braced on the head-rest of her chair, straightened up but didn't break eye contact. 'A very nice ear,' he said, his voice doing almost as much damage to her nervous system as his warm breath had. 'I could eat it.'

'You really don't have to do this, you know.' She could barely hear her own voice above the clamour of her thudding heart.

'Do?'

The circles of colour that appeared on the apples of her cheeks looked feverishly bright against her marble pallor.

'Say…stuff. I really don't expect it, you know, just because we slept together once,' she assured him earnestly. '*All right*,' she conceded, 'twice. But you can't really count the last time.'

Her reassurance wiped the smile right off his face. 'You can't… Why?' A nerve clenched hard in his lean cheek as he brought his hand along the side of her jaw. 'Did you have your fingers crossed?'

Scarlet felt the heat rush to her cheeks. She glanced over her shoulder, aware that their conversation was a little personal for so public a place.

Their new seats were directly adjacent to a group of men who all wore rugby kit; the noise they were making made it unlikely they were going to hear anything she said. One of their number she had exchanged a few words with earlier caught her eye and winked.

Scarlet responded to his, 'Hello, lovely girl,' with a grin and a wave before turning back to Roman.

'It's not going to happen again,' she declared in a fierce undertone.

While she spoke he maintained an expression of polite disbelief that made her want to hit him.

'Because you don't want it to?' he suggested in a light conversational tone.

'I've not given it much thought.' Lies didn't get much bigger or more improbable.

'Sure you haven't, as in you've not thought about much else.' He shook his head, the cynical twist to his wide, sensual mouth becoming more pronounced as he looked across at her miserable face. 'Grow up, Scarlet,' he advised tautly. 'There's absolutely no way we could share a bedroom and nothing happen,' he imparted simply.

The thing was his confidence was fully justified. 'That might be true,' she admitted bitterly. 'But I'm not sharing a bedroom with you so we won't find out!'

'I've already explained the sleeping arrangements to my parents.'

'Then you'll have to unexplain them.'

'I can't do that.'

'Why not?'

'Because they expect an engaged couple to sleep in the same bed.'

She stilled and lost what little colour she had. 'What did you say?'

'You heard what I said, Scarlet.'

'Why would your parents think we were engaged?' she enquired in a deceptively mild tone.

'Because that's what I told them.'

She loosed an incredulous peal of laughter. 'Have you lost your mind?' she exploded.

Roman's dark lashes lifted and his eyes glittered with an anger to match her own. 'If I have the blame can be laid directly at your door. Mixed signals don't cover it,' he declared. 'You introduced this ridiculous no-touch policy while at the same time you look at me with those big hungry eyes. It's enough to send the sanest man born round the bed.'

'I do *not* have hungry eyes!'

His brows lifted. 'Sure, and you just hate making love with me. The screams are actually a sign of how much you hate it.'

'I don't scream!' she choked.

'Like a banshee, but I like a woman who can let herself go.'

'You,' she told him in a voice that quivered with outrage, 'are crude and vulgar. A woman would have to be mad to marry you.'

'And are you?'

She stilled, her wide eyes fixed on his face. 'What do you mean?' she asked hoarsely.

'Are you going to marry me, Scarlet?'

'I thought it was a done deal,' she remarked bitterly.

He gave a sardonic lopsided smile but didn't reply.

'You're thinking of Sam?' she suggested.

He opened his mouth as if to say something, then closed it again. When he did speak he appeared to be choosing his words with care. 'I think he would approve. A proper family…maybe a brother or sister.'

She heard the rather worrying sound of slightly hysterical laughter. 'You want a baby?'

He looked mildly surprised. 'Don't you?' he returned.

'Yes,' she heard herself reply. 'Eventually,' she added, trying to retrieve the situation. 'I'm sure you'd get the same answer from most women.'

'I'm not asking most women to marry me, I'm asking you, Scarlet, and I'm still waiting for an answer.'

You had to respect the man for not pretending he loved her, she thought. People in arranged marriages sometimes fell in love and even when they didn't they had happy marriages.

My God, Scarlet, you're talking yourself into this, aren't you?

It would be mad to marry without love.

'Yes, I'll marry you.'

A smile of pure male triumph spread across his face. 'Excellent.' He got to his feet and Scarlet saw that Sam was awake and had his nose pressed to the window. 'Come on, Sam, you'll get a better view of the chopper up there,' he said, taking the little boy's hand.

'I want to fly in a chopper.'

'And you will, Sam,' his father promised.

Just like that, she thought, watching as he led the boy away. She hadn't expected a fanfare or champagne, but *excellent*?

Dear God, what have I done?

CHAPTER FOURTEEN

ROMAN had not exaggerated the remoteness or inaccessibility of the O'Hagan estate. They had driven four miles from the village before they finally reached the gated entrance. They had been travelling along what Roman referred to as the drive, but it wasn't like any drive Scarlet had seen, for at least ten minutes now, and there was still no sign of a house or for that matter a person!

Occasionally there was a break in the trees flanking the driveway affording breath-taking vistas over parkland towards the mountains or sea, and sometimes both. Under normal circumstances Scarlet would have wanted to get out of the car and spend time appreciating the magnificent scenery.

These were not normal circumstances!

She sighed as the next bend revealed no end to the journey. She was still dreading the entire 'meet the in-laws' thing, but she had reached the point where she wanted it over and done with. The reality could not be worse than what she was imagining...*could it*? At least Sam was no longer grouching—he had fallen asleep a couple of miles back, but this almost guaranteed he would be incredibly cranky when he woke up.

'What if they hate me?' They would like Sam. Everyone liked Sam.

Roman slid an amused sideways look at her tense face. 'Well, naturally I will cast you off like a smelly sock.'

'I don't smell!' she protested.

His nostrils flared. 'You do,' he contradicted throatily. 'I can smell you on my skin after we've made love.'

She was overpoweringly conscious of the fluid heat in the pit of her belly. 'Like that's happened such a lot,' she retorted, and shifted her position to lessen the pressure on her sensitised breasts.

'It will,' he declared arrogantly.

Now she really was a basket case.

Eyes fixed glassily on the narrow track ahead, Scarlet kept her tongue firmly between her teeth. She had learnt she could say some very reckless things when consumed by lust and right now she was shaking with it! She still was, only hopefully less obviously so, when he spoke a few moments later.

'Why do you crave approval?'

'I don't,' she denied indignantly.

'The only person you need to please is me.' His dark-lashed midnight eyes only touched her face for a split second but it was long enough to send a lick of heat through her body.

'And do I? Because you have no idea how much I would *not* care if—'

'Yes, you do please me...*very much*.'

Scarlet's audible gasp filled the short pause that followed his earthy admission.

She screwed her eyes up tight. 'I *really* wish you wouldn't say things like that.'

'The truth bothers you?'

'*You* bother me!' she exploded resentfully.

'Hold on,' she heard him say.

Scarlet opened her eyes and saw there was a horse just ahead. The rider, a female, twisted around in her saddle as she heard the car engine. Apparently recognising Roman, she started waving madly at them.

Scarlet turned her head, but Roman wasn't looking at her, he was looking at the figure on the horse and he was grinning, an uncomplicated grin of pleasure.

'Someone you know?'

Roman didn't reply; instead he pulled the car up on the grass verge.

'I won't be long.' He was already out of the door when he put his head back inside. 'Has it occurred to you they are probably equally concerned about what you'll think of them?'

'Your family?'

'Our family.'

She lowered her eyes, confused by the possessive glow in his dark eyes. 'Because I'm so very scary.'

Despite her sarcastic retort, actually his comment had made her feel a lot more positive. He was right—what did it matter if Sam was cranky or she looked like an unmade bed? The big picture wasn't about first impressions.

'Scary?' The husky rasp of his voice brought her eyes back to his face. One corner of his mouth lifted in a crooked smile, and there was a warmth in his eyes that made her heart beat faster. 'I think you're delicious.'

Delicious!

The upward surge in her spirits and confidence lasted until she saw that the person on the horse had swept off her riding hat; wavy shoulder-length chestnut hair fell free, and it shone in the weak sun. She lifted the waves off her face with a gloved hand and Scarlet could see she was very pretty.

As Roman approached the horse began to dance around in an alarming fashion—at least it seemed alarming to Scarlet. Casually the rider controlled it. Roman patted the quivering animal's neck as he came level with them.

The rider leaned down in her saddle and, with a hand

behind Roman's dark head, pressed her mouth to his. While Scarlet sat and watched the woman talking in an animated fashion to Roman the tight feeling in her chest got tighter and tighter.

She couldn't remember Roman ever looking that relaxed and happy with her. Several times she threw back his head and laughed out loud.

'That was lucky,' he remarked as he slid back into the car and turned on the ignition. 'I was hoping to bump into Sally.'

The name made Scarlet stiffen. It was several moments before she could trust herself to speak.

'*Sally,*' she repeated in a conversational tone. 'Would that be the same Sally who left you at the altar?'

'All forgotten.'

Scarlet smiled, her eyes trained on her intertwined white-knuckled fingers. 'How civilised.' The primitive emotions she was experiencing were anything but!

'Well, we're all grown-ups aren't we? And life's far too short to hold grudges. Do you ride?'

Scarlet's head came up. 'Horses?'

'Horses,' he agreed, looking amused by her horrified expression.

'I can't ride.'

'You'll be able to see the house around the next bend. Pity you can't ride—you could have come out with me and Sally tomorrow morning.'

'You're going riding with her?'

'Is that a problem?'

Scarlet released a slow, fractured hiss. 'You bet it's a problem.'

Roman glanced at her rigid profile and stopped the car. He released his seat belt and turned his body to face her. 'Do you mind elaborating on that statement?'

'The fact I need to just goes to prove what a totally insensitive bastard you are. Damn!' she cursed, tears starting in her eyes.

'Let me.' Roman leaned across her, his arms brushing against her aching breasts as he released the seat-belt catch her trembling fingers had been unable to cope with. His warmth, the scent of his body, his nearness—they all conspired to fill Scarlet with an aching longing that went bone-deep.

She held herself rigid until he had straightened up.

'So what's the problem?' he asked, in a *here-we-go-again* tone that sent her temper through the roof.

'We'll put all that guff you gave me about fidelity to one side for a minute, because I didn't believe a word of it anyhow,' she revealed contemptuously.

'Is that fact?' Low and without expression, his voice still managed to leave her in no doubt that he didn't like what he was hearing.

Her chin went up defiantly. If she started screening everything she said for his approval rating she'd probably never open her mouth again.

'There are limits to even *my* gullibility, you know.'

His nostrils flared as he sucked in a breath; his golden chiselled features were a taut mask of anger. She felt despair as she realised that even now his compelling male beauty had the power to touch her deeply.

'But not your stupidity.'

'*My* stupidity? You're the one who expects your family to take us getting married seriously when the moment you arrive you're riding off into the hills with the love of your life!'

'Are we talking about Sally?'

'How many loves of your life are there?'

He gave her a black look. 'Only one.'

The crushing confirmation was like a body-blow. Her pride wouldn't let him see how much she was hurting. 'Am I supposed to turn a blind eye?'

'To what?'

'*To what?* You kissed her!' She stuffed her fist into her mouth to stop the sob that was trying to escape.

'And you didn't like that?'

Scarlet lifted her head and her eyes skated warily across his lean face; he no longer looked angry. It was hard to read from his apparently relaxed expression what he was feeling.

'Would you like it if I went around kissing my old boy-friends? Daft question, I don't suppose you'd even notice,' she ended on a self-pitying sniff. With a deep sigh she closed her eyes. 'God, this was *such* a stupid idea. I don't know how I let you talk me into it?'

'*I would notice.*'

Her eyes widened at the aggressive declaration. 'You would?'

His fingers curved around her jaw, turning her face up to his. 'And I wouldn't like it.' His dark eyes shimmered. 'Actually I *wouldn't like it* quite a lot.'

Her heart started beating very fast. 'What would you do?' she whispered.

A slow wolfish smile spread across his dark, lean face. 'I'd throttle him...just a little, you understand, but enough so that he got the point.'

Suddenly her throat was so dry she could hardly speak. His primitive statement should have appalled her and here she was *excited*...and trying very hard not to let him see *how* excited.

'The point being?'

'That my wife is off limits.'

'I thought we were grown-ups,' she reminded him with

a disgruntled glare. 'Besides, I don't see why I shouldn't kiss whoever I want—you do.'

He laughed. 'That wasn't a kiss…' She read his intent before his head lowered. 'This,' he told her throatily, 'is a kiss.'

With a sigh she leaned back in her seat. Her lips felt tender and her body was gently thrumming with thwarted desire. It had been a kiss, but she had wanted more.

'You know it's very, *very* hard to stop kissing you once I start.' It was some small comfort that his voice reflected some of the strain and frustration she was experiencing.

'Then why did you stop?'

Roman jerked his head towards the back seat where Sam was sleepily rubbing his eyes. 'We have an audience.'

'I want a drink,' Sam announced loudly.

'And you shall have one,' Roman promised. 'Look, there's the house,' he said, starting up the engine.

'It looks like something out of a Jane Austen book,' Scarlet said in an awed voice as the big building loomed ahead of them. She turned reproachful eyes on him. 'You said it wasn't very big.'

'It's only bricks and mortar—don't let the size intimidate you.'

Easy for someone who had been brought up here to say. 'Is it very old?'

'Late Georgian,' Roman explained. 'With some rather ugly Victorian additions. Ask my father about the history…you'll regret it, but you'll score plenty of brownie points.'

'Is that what you want me to do?'

He scanned her pale, tense face with wide, anxious eyes and he exhaled deeply. 'For God's sake, will you stop worrying about what other people want and do what you damned well want?'

His anger made her blink, but it seemed to drain away as fast as it had erupted. He reached across and brushed a strand of hair from her cheek; she shivered as his fingertips lightly grazed her skin. 'Do you like it?'

'Like?' she repeated, fighting the compulsion to rub her cheek against his hand.

'The house.'

'Oh, right…yes…' She pulled back and his hand fell away. 'Like wasn't the right word,' she modified. 'It's big and very beautiful.' *Just like you.* 'I suppose people had lots of children in those days.'

'Mum is trying to persuade Dad to retire to Italy. She's talking of renovating one of the estate cottages for when they come over. She thinks this place is too big for them now.'

Scarlet looked up at the daunting façade and tried but failed to imagine Sam watching Saturday morning cartoons on the telly there…she couldn't. 'I can see her point.' She stiffened as two figures began to walk across the forecourt.

'Oh, God…'

She was in too much of a panic to notice when Roman left the car without comment. He opened the passenger door with Sam secured against his hip with his free arm. He looked at her pale face.

'They'll love you.'

'Says you,' she hissed back, wishing she could share even a fraction of his daunting assurance.

Roman seemed to lack any insight into her feelings. Didn't he understand what it felt like to be here under sufferance, the woman that came with the grandchild they wanted—a package deal?

She slid out of her seat and pinned a smile on her face,

very conscious that his parents were now close enough to hear what they were saying.

Even so they wouldn't have heard what Roman said when he bent close, his lips almost brushing her ear; she barely caught the husky words herself.

'Well, if they don't love you, remember I do, and that's what counts.'

All Scarlet had time to do was shoot him a stunned slack-jawed look before they were knee-deep in hugs and introductions.

It was ironic considering how much she had been dreading this meeting, and how carefully she had planned what she was going to say down to the last detail and inflection, that when it arrived she didn't have the faintest idea what she said or whom she said it to!

The whole thing passed by in a blur, a dream. Her mind was elsewhere.

He said he loved me.

It was possible that saying it out loud might make it seem more real. But Scarlet retained just enough self-control to stop herself trying out the theory.

'I hope you like the room.'

Scarlet smiled a little vaguely. *'Room…?'*

'I hope you like this room,' Natalia repeated patiently.

'Of course, it's a lovely room.' She spared the beautifully furnished bedroom a cursory glance, which lingered longest on the bed she was to share with Roman.

'Sam is in the connecting room—I thought that would be best.'

'Sam!' Scarlet looked around the room, alarm jolting her belatedly to an alert state. 'Where is he?'

Natalia looked at her strangely. 'He has gone to look at

the puppies in the kitchen, remember? You said it would be all right. I can get him if you like.'

Deeply embarrassed, Scarlet blushed. 'Of course…no, that's all right. He's always wanted a dog.'

'All children like puppies and Alice is with him. He'll be fine.'

Alice, Scarlet seemed to recall, dredging through her vague memories of the past few minutes, was the tall blonde who had been introduced as Roman's PA. Roman's father had turned out to have an appearance that matched his intimidating reputation: a big, burly man with a shock of grey hair and an abrupt manner.

'Yes, I'm sure he will.'

'You must be tired after the journey. If you'd like to lie down for a while before dinner you may. Hopefully Luca will be here by then and you'll be able to meet all the family.'

There was only one member of the O'Hagan family she wanted to see at that moment and he was closeted in the study taking a vital call.

She didn't think much of his priorities!

'I am tired,' Scarlet agreed, relieved to have a legitimate reason to explain away behaviour that had to seem pretty bizarre to the other woman. 'Maybe I'll have a shower, or a walk.'

She doubted whether ten cold showers were going to make her any more articulate. It was so typical of Roman to say something like that and then get himself called away.

'Well, I'll be in the drawing room if you want me and I'm sure Roman won't be long,' Natalia said as if reading her mind. 'Would you like some tea brought up to your room?'

'No, thank you, I might wait for Roman.'

CHAPTER FIFTEEN

SCARLET did wait but, contrary to his mother's prediction, Roman *was* long, or at least it seemed that way to Scarlet. She had unpacked her clothes and Sam's in the pretty adjoining room, which looked suspiciously as though it had been recently decorated. Someone, probably their hostess, had gone to a lot of trouble to make them feel welcome and comfortable. She felt a pang of guilt when she realised how ungrateful she must have seemed.

She reached the point where she had half convinced herself he hadn't said anything at all and she had imagined the whole thing when she decided enough was enough. If she sat here any longer, her thoughts going around in circles, she'd go quietly barmy, and she was neglecting her duty as a parent.

She was pretty sure that Sam would be where the puppies were and they were in the kitchen.

Scarlet found the warm cosy room with its original range and modern day appliances, and tried to apologise to Alice for Sam being a nuisance. But Alice, clearly not immune to the charm of his big brown eyes, announced that Sam wasn't bothering her and they were enjoying themselves.

The cook had given them the run of the kitchen so long as they cleaned up after themselves and Alice, with Sam's help, planned to make a batch of scones.

Helping involved a lot of flour and Scarlet left him happily up to his armpits in the stuff.

* * *

Making her way back from the domestic offices to the main part of the rambling house was not as easy as it sounded. When Scarlet found herself back in the boot room for the second time she began to think she might be doomed to wander the below-stairs corridors for ever.

Maybe it was someone's way of telling her that was where she belonged, she thought with an ironic smile. She certainly felt a lot more comfortable in the cosy old-fashioned kitchen than she expected to upstairs in the drawing room.

When she did eventually find herself in the main hallway she wasn't entirely sure how she got there. Her heels were noisy on the gleaming wooden floor as she slowed her pace outside the study door behind which she had seen Roman disappear.

Perhaps Roman wasn't in there. Perhaps he had finished and was even now waiting for her upstairs. The possibility made her heartbeat quicken—and her stride.

It was Sam's name that slowed her down. She could hear voices coming through the slightly open door. She stopped pretending to herself she wasn't eavesdropping when she identified the distinctive sound of Roman's deep voice.

Even this far away it had the ability to raise goose-bumps on her skin. Her weakness brought a smile to her lips; this faded when Roman's voice was closely followed by the deep rumble of Finn O'Hagan's voice raised loudly in anger.

'I suppose it's better late than never...' she heard him observe grudgingly. 'A man should never feel ashamed of his own child.'

Shock held Scarlet frozen to the spot. Had Roman told his father he was ashamed of Sam? Had all the things he'd said been a lie? It was hard for her to believe this, but it was equally hard to read his comment any other way.

'When I look at that poor innocent babe I'm ashamed.

Ashamed that I raised a man who can't see beyond his own selfish pleasure.'

Scarlet flinched as there was the sound of something falling...breaking...and Finn's terse instruction to, 'Leave the damned thing alone. Someone will pick it up later.'

'I'm ashamed of you, I'm ashamed I'm your father.'

Scarlet, who now recognised with a sick feeling what was happening, pressed her hand to her mouth.

'I'm sorry to be such a disappointment to you, Father.' In contrast to his father's voice, Roman's was rigidly controlled. 'You shouldn't get excited, Father.'

'I'm not excited, I'm *disgusted*.'

Without thinking about what she was doing, acting purely on an instinct that told her she couldn't let Roman take the blame for something that he was innocent of, Scarlet stepped through the door into the room.

The morning sun was streaming in through the windows of the big book-lined room, and, combined with the glow from the blazing open log fire in the vast carved stone fireplace, it should have made for a warm, cosy atmosphere. But inside the atmosphere was ice.

The two big men, both standing with a large oak desk between them, didn't notice her.

'Sit down, father, and let's discuss this rationally.' From where she was standing she could see the strain in Roman's face. His strongly etched profile was taut and each angle and hollow of his face sharply defined.

'It doesn't matter how *rationally* we discuss it. It's not going to alter the fact that because of you a woman lost her life giving birth to your son.'

A sudden calmness that came from knowing what she had to do settled over Scarlet.

'No!' Her soft voice had a bell-like clarity as she stepped forward into the room. 'This has to stop now.'

The two men turned in unison. 'Scarlet, leave it,' Roman said, moving to block her impetuous entrance.

She shook her head and braced herself against his upper arms with her hands, but he still frustrated her efforts to reach his father, physically blocking her with his own body. Scarlet felt the iron-hard muscles in his well-developed upper arms clench beneath her fingers. Their eyes meshed.

'This isn't right.'

'This isn't your problem, Scarlet.'

'Maybe it isn't, but I'm not going to leave it. I've left it too long already,' she reflected grimly.

'You're defending my son?'

'Well, someone has to,' Scarlet said, stepping back from Roman because there was no way she was going through him.

'After what he did to your own sister.'

The scornful recrimination in the older man's voice brought a flush to her cheeks. 'The point is, he didn't.'

The older man shook his head impatiently. 'Is this what he's told you, girl?'

Roman's deep voice cut angrily across his father. 'Her name is Scarlet, Father. If you want to vent your anger on anyone, I'm here. Leave her out of it.'

The eyes of father and son clashed for a moment. Finn O'Hagan was the first to look away with a slight nod of acknowledgement.

Scarlet's chin lifted. 'I can defend myself,' she told Roman. Then turned to his father. 'Nobody tells me what to think, Mr O'Hagan,' she declared proudly.

'Fine words. You'll be telling me next he isn't the father.'

'Roman is Sam's father,' she admitted.

Roman's father gave an impatient snort. 'Exactly, there's nothing more to be said. The facts speak for themselves.'

'No, actually, they don't, Mr O'Hagan. Roman didn't seduce my sister. None of it was an accident.'

'What are you talking about, Scarlet?' Roman asked.

'Abby *wanted* a baby.'

'I know.'

'No,' she interrupted loudly. 'You don't know. Abby planned to have a baby and she picked you out as the father.'

'Picked me?' Roman shook his head. 'What are you talking about, Scarlet?'

'Abby picked you out to be the father of her baby. I think having a child became an obsession.' Her trembling lower lip caught between her teeth, she lowered her eyes guiltily.

She couldn't bring herself to look at him. She could only imagine how angry and disgusted he must be feeling and how she was the natural focus for his anger. She couldn't expect him to understand that telling him the truth was a betrayal of her sister's memory.

She took a deep breath before continuing.

'Abby told me shortly before her death that she planned it all. She spiked his drink and…she made sure that any…any *precautions* didn't work. She never had any intention that he would be involved with Sam,' she admitted miserably. 'The morning after,' she added, determined now she had begun to make a clean breast of it, 'to make sure Roman wouldn't suspect anything she told him that nothing had happened, that he had fallen asleep.'

There was a thunderstruck silence. Finn O'Hagan stared at her, then turned to his son. 'My God, can this be true?'

Roman, his dark shadowed eyes still on Scarlet's face, didn't respond to the incredulous question. His impenetrable expression made it impossible to know what to read into his silence.

There was a husky note of appeal in Scarlet's voice as she addressed her words directly to a stony-faced Roman.

'Abby wasn't a bad person,' she faltered huskily. 'She'd had a couple of relationships over the previous year that ended badly. I think she thought that she'd never find a man to love but she wanted a baby.'

'And her solution was to get a man drunk and sleep with him…?'

Scarlet could hear precious little of the understanding she'd been praying for in his voice. She felt her throat close over with unshed tears and drew a deep, slow breath.

'Please don't think badly of her!' she pleaded. Tears stood out in her eyes as she turned towards the door. 'And, Mr O'Hagan, nobody has told you, but it wasn't Roman who called off the wedding to Sally, she did. She ran off with the best man. So you see this isn't the first time you've blamed Roman for something that wasn't his fault. I'd say he's earned the benefit of the doubt…wouldn't you?

'If I were you I'd be grateful I had a son like Roman, not spend my time looking for things to be mean to him about.' She barely managed to get the rebuke out before her self-control snapped and she fled from the room, tears streaming down her cheeks.

For several minutes after she'd gone neither man moved. It was Finn O'Hagan who finally broke the tableau. He looked at his son's profile without comment and went over to the bureau. He poured a generous measure of Irish whiskey from an unopened bottle and drained the glass in one swallow. With a sigh he poured a second, refilled his own and approached his son.

'Is it true about Sally?'

Roman gave a shrug. 'It was a long time ago.'

'I assume that was a yes. It would seem that I owe you an apology.'

Roman's fingers curled around the glass extended to him. 'You thought I'd been a selfish bastard. I thought I'd been a selfish bastard.' His powerful shoulders lifted before he raised the glass to his lips. 'Forget it,' he advised.

'That took some guts...coming in here like she did.'

'You think?'

'Don't you?'

'This isn't about courage,' Roman began forcefully before visibly restraining himself. He ran a hand down his jaw.

'What is it about, Roman?' his father asked quietly. With a groan he lowered himself into a chair. 'I'm as stiff as a damned board,' he complained. 'Your mother might be right, maybe I do need a bit of sun in my old age.' His eyes followed the panther-like, prowling progress of his son as he trod a path down the length of the room and back again.

'The girl must have been torn; it can't be an easy thing it's her sister.'

Roman's dark eyes flared. 'And I'm her bloody husband...or I will be,' he growled, banging the glass down on the desk.

'Oh, that's still on, is it?'

Roman turned on him in a flash. 'What the hell is that supposed to mean? Are you saying I shouldn't marry her?'

Finn appeared to consider the question. 'Well, maybe you could do better.' He silently counted to three before his son exploded.

'*Better?*' he repeated, his eyes narrowed to menacing icy slits. 'I don't want *better*, I want Scarlet.'

Finn smiled up at his glowering son. 'Don't tell me, boy, tell her.'

It was about half an hour later that there was a knock on her bedroom door. Scarlet, who was lying full length on the bed, rolled over and tried to smooth down her hair. It was going to be hard to explain away her bedraggled appearance, she thought, grimacing as she examined the marks twenty minutes of unrestrained weeping had left on her face in the mirror.

'I'll be right there,' she called, sliding her legs off the bed.

The door opened. 'Don't bother.'

Scarlet just sat there awkwardly as Roman came into the room and closed the door behind him.

It was a meeting she had been dreading but one she knew she had to face some time or other. At least now there were no lies or half-told truths between them. A relationship that was built on love could survive the truth. If it couldn't, maybe it wasn't worth saving.

Total rubbish! the voice in her head replied in response to this fatalistic maxim. *Only an idiot stands there and lets their future go down the toilet without at least trying to stop it.*

'I know you must hate me at the moment,' she said, studying the polished floor. Her hair fell forward, the glossy bangs hiding her face and exposing the nape of her neck.

His piercing glance touched the top of her bowed glossy head. His mouth twisted. 'Do I?'

'And I don't blame you,' she hastened to add. 'But I really hope that later on when things are less…*raw* you'll be able to see… It was wrong not to tell you, very wrong—I can see that now.'

'Why tell me now, Scarlet?' Roman demanded, dragging a hand through his dark hair.

'Because I heard your father. I couldn't let him talk to you like that. I couldn't let you take the blame for something when you were innocent.'

'Why not?'

She shook her head. 'I just couldn't.'

'It hadn't bothered you up to that point,' he reminded her. 'You let me…hell, you *listened* and were incredibly supportive to me while I beat myself up, and you didn't say a word. Not one bloody word,' he reiterated in disbelief. 'Did it give you some sort of kick to see me eaten up with guilt?'

Unable to bear the anger in his dark, hostile eyes, she looked away.

'Well, did it?' he demanded harshly.

Scarlet looked up and, numb with misery, shook her head.

The sight of the tears rolling down her cheeks seemed to inflame him even farther. 'And there was me unable to believe how you could be so generous in forgiving me.'

Scarlet bit her lips and his lips twisted into a smile that was so bitter and bleak it made her wince. Those same lips had kissed her so beautifully, with such passion, with such tenderness.

'Wondering,' he continued in a voice that throbbed with bitter self-derision, 'what I did to deserve someone so charitable and sweet.'

A strangled sob escaped her lips before she pressed her hand over her mouth.

Roman watched her chin fall to her chest in an attitude of abject misery and his dark features contorted. Scarlet didn't see that or the hand he had stretched out towards her before letting it fall.

'Hell!' he ejaculated rawly as he began to restively pace up and down the room. At the far end of the room he twisted back to face her. *'You must hate me.'*

Scarlet blinked away the hot tears that filled her eyes, her throat felt so emotionally tight she could hardly breathe. She shook her head in denial.

'I love you, Roman.'

He stopped dead.

'I wanted to tell you about Abby.'

'But you managed to stop yourself,' he cut back with dark irony.

'I couldn't tell you what Abby did without—'

'Speaking ill of the dead?' He shook his head. 'That doesn't work.'

'But it's the truth,' she protested feebly. 'At first I didn't think there was any point telling you. Later I wanted to protect you from the truth, and I was worried that, if you knew, you might not feel the same way about Sam.'

'*Protect me?*'

Head bowed, she didn't look at him. 'I'll explain to your parents that this is my fault. At least you didn't send out the invitations this time.'

'What the hell are you talking about?' he snarled.

'Well, obviously we can't get married now, not even for Sam.' He was never going to forgive her. Later she would feel regret and pain; right now she felt numb. It was a blessing really.

'I was never marrying you for Sam.'

Her head lifted and what she saw in his face made her heart thud.

'When you said that you loved me, Roman, did you mean it?'

He stilled. '*Love you?*' His eyes closed and he drew a deep shuddering breath.

'Or maybe you did,' she put in quickly—she didn't want to hear him say anything that would spoil that brief perfect moment when she had thought he loved her. 'But now you don't—?'

His eyes opened. 'You don't switch off love like a tap.'

She blinked in bewilderment. 'But you despise me, you'll never forgive me.'

'Do I look that much of a fool?' he demanded, sweeping a strong hand through his dark hair. 'No, don't answer that, I know I do. I…I say things when I'm angry,' he revealed awkwardly. 'I was totally unprepared to hear what you had to say. It's not an ego-enhancing thing to learn that you were used as breeding stock.'

'I know.'

'I'm perfectly aware that you were in an impossible position,' he admitted.

'I should have told you.'

He shrugged. 'It wasn't the fact you didn't tell me that made me so angry,' he revealed. 'It was the fact you thought you *couldn't* tell me, the fact that you thought anything could change the way I feel about Sam.'

'I'm sorry,' she whispered.

A sudden grin spread across his face as he crossed the room to her, his long legs covering the space in two seconds flat. He took her face between his hands.

'Don't do humble, Scarlet; it doesn't suit you.'

'You're not angry with me?'

He shook his head. 'It's not like I haven't been guilty of my share of economy in the truth department. I'm capable of cynical manipulation.'

'Who were you manipulating?'

'You,' he admitted. 'I asked you to marry me because of Sam. I calculated that you were more likely to say yes if I played the happy family card, rather than admit the truth.'

Scarlet ran a finger down the thin white line on his cheek and felt his big body shudder. With a muffled groan he caught her hand and pressed an open-mouthed kiss into the palm.

'What was the truth, Roman?' she whispered huskily.

His lips lifted from her skin, but he retained her hand,

rubbing it up and down his jaw. She could feel the prickle of the dark shadowy stubble.

'The truth is I had fallen in love with you, my brave, bolshy and absolutely beautiful Scarlet.' The light of undisguised adoration in his face sent a thrill of wonder through her body. 'I have been half off my head, unable to think about anything else,' he admitted rawly.

'I never guessed!'

'Dear God, I thought I was being obvious enough. Do you actually think I'd travel on a ferry for anyone but you?'

A small gurgle of laughter left her lips before her expression grew grave. 'You miscalculated, Roman.'

His wary eyes scanned her solemn face. *'I did?'*

'The truth would have been much more effective,' she told him simply.

With a smile of fierce relief he drew her to him. He kissed her with a hunger and desperation that made her senses spin.

'I think we should make it a rule to tell each other the truth in future,' he said when his mouth finally lifted.

'But we can tell the odd white lie to other people?'

'Did you have something specific in mind, *cara*?'

'Well, would it be so bad if we made up a little excuse for not going back downstairs straight away?' she wondered with an innocent smile.

'I never need an excuse to make love to my woman,' he declared with breath-taking arrogance. 'And, in addition, in Italy it is common practice to retire into a darkened room in the middle of the day. Siesta is a very civilised custom,' he rasped.

'True, but we're not in Italy.'

'But I'm half Italian,' he reminded her as he scooped her up into his arms and carried her to the bed. 'You'll enjoy being married to an Italian,' he promised.

'I'm beginning to think you could be right,' she agreed with a blissful smile.

'I always am.'

Just this once Scarlet decided she would let Roman get away with this outrageous claim. After all, there would be plenty of other chances for her to point out the error of his ways. Not that she wanted to change her Italian lover; she liked him just the way he was!

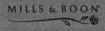

FREE
4 BOOKS
AND A SURPRISE GIFT!

We would like to take this opportunity to thank you for reading this Mills & Boon® book by offering you the chance to take FOUR more specially selected titles from the Modern Romance™ series absolutely FREE! We're also making this offer to introduce you to the benefits of the Reader Service™—

- ★ FREE home delivery
- ★ FREE monthly Newsletter
- ★ FREE gifts and competitions
- ★ Exclusive Reader Service discount
- ★ Books available before they're in the shops

Accepting these FREE books and gift places you under no obligation to buy; you may cancel at any time, even after receiving your free shipment. Simply complete your details below and return the entire page to the address below. *You don't even need a stamp!*

YES! Please send me 4 free Modern Romance™ books and a surprise gift. I understand that unless you hear from me, I will receive 6 superb new titles every month for just £2.69 each, postage and packing free. I am under no obligation to purchase any books and may cancel my subscription at any time. The free books and gift will be mine to keep in any case.

P4ZEF

Ms/Mrs/Miss/Mr .... Initials ....

BLOCK CAPITALS PLEASE

Surname ....

Address ....

....

.... Postcode ....

Send this whole page to:
UK: FREEPOST CN81, Croydon, CR9 3WZ
EIRE: PO Box 4546, Kilcock, County Kildare (stamp required)